CRYSTAL QUEST

*Hunting through time and space
to get the zodiac crystals first!*

PART FOUR
Atlantis Betrayed

David Johnson

Pen Press

First published in Great Britain by
Indepenpress Publishing Ltd
25 Eastern Place
Brighton
BN2 1GJ

ISBN13: 978-1-906710-39-2

Printed and bound in the UK

A catalogue record of this book is available from
the British Library

Cover design by Kate Larsen

This book is dedicated to family,
Chris, Vicky, Paul, James, Sally-Ann, Ethel and Alan.

To Kate
for interpreting my wild ideas into artwork once again.

To Luke
for his ceaseless enthusiasm to all things Sci-Fi.

To Matt
for his unrivalled fiction knowledge and support.

About the author

David Johnson lives in Devizes, Wiltshire, UK, with his family and friends. His love of travel, history, Sci-Fi, films and current affairs has all contributed to this story. His fascination with local places like Stonehenge, Avebury, and neighbouring Glastonbury has been central to establishing key elements of the story.

He uses local places he knows, overseas places he has visited and historic events he is interested in to blend into this fast-paced young adults Sci-Fi quest.

He has also been a guest speaker at International writing events abroad and spoken at schools in the UK, New Zealand and Eire.

Picture shows David Johnson exploring temples and Colossi of Ramses II at Abu Simbel in Egypt.

The story so far…

A series of dramatic events have hurled twelve-year-old amateur scientist James Lightwater, on a quest to stop the evil Dark Zodiac secret society and their alien masters from taking over the world and using humans as food!

The schoolboy's perilous quest began just days ago, when he accidentally sucked Maximus-Prime (Max), an ugly living computer from 100 years in the future, through a doorway in time. A time door opened by the mysterious black gas used in James's everlasting light bulb experiment.

Pressured by Max to embark on the secret quest, James must prevent the Dark Zodiac from getting 12 zodiac crystals in the correct order, which are hidden throughout time.

Max reveals that ten thousand years ago the leaders of Atlantis deliberately hid the powerful crystals. And the coded message on an ancient stone tablet tells that it is James's destiny to go after the crystals!

Using his own time travel equipment and a stolen alien combat suit, James makes a time suit and starts on the perilous quest to get the crystals first. To help him, Max gives James a talking, cricket ball sized location device called TALON (Tracking And Locating Organic Navigator). Inside it there is a tiny living brain and an ancient Egyptian coin showing the coded locations of all 12 crystals.

However the Dark Zodiac relentlessly uses their own time travel craft to hunt down TALON and the brave boy.

In a series of battles, James has already succeeded in getting the first four crystals – (Aquarius) from ancient Stonehenge, (Gemini) from Egypt before the pyramids were built, (Libra) while causing the great fire of London in 1666 and (Aries) destroying Pompeii in 79 AD.

He has also gained valuable allies in his travels. The ancient British High Priest *Davius,* from Stonehenge, and Max have been forced to flee their own time periods to join James in the present.

However most disturbing of all, James has discovered that he can control and use crystals; but that they can influence his thoughts and unleash the darker side of his personality. Even if he gets all the crystals first, will he be able to control them, or will he succumb to their power and become a deadly menace to the world as well?

In the most recent climatic battle, James destroys the Dark Zodiac in their secret underground base and stops the aliens' plans. However he wrongly believes that he has also killed all the aliens in the underground battle. What he does not know is that they have a separate base elsewhere on the earth.

Now convinced that he no longer needs to finish the quest, James is intent on travelling into the future to see if stopping the quest will alter the course of human history. And if it has, he is determined to risk going back in time to ancient Atlantis to get all the crystals in one go, rather than finish the quest!

Now read on…

Chapter 1

"We need humans for food and the Earth as a base to build our slave armies!" bellowed the alien leader at the top of its telepathic voice. The other aliens floated around it in wild excitement, declaring their agreement in telepathic unison.

Their collective thoughts echoed throughout their secret Headquarters.

They were in a large chamber at the centre of the underground headquarters which was connected to a network of other tunnels. It was like a vast insect nest with a large metallic craft at its centre. The chamber contained a massive transparent tank which extended to the ceiling. Lots of twisted tubes and cables of all sizes extended from the circular tank. The tank was filled to the ceiling with swirling yellow and green liquid. Inside it seven aliens swam slowly in the green liquid; their thoughts flowing between one another like sparks. They were like large, jelly fish, each one twice the size of a man. Their tentacles writhed snake-like in the unearthly liquid. The leader (who James had encountered before) floated dominantly in the middle of the circle of other aliens.

"The Dark Zodiac headquarters has been totally destroyed by the boy. All records of who he is and where he lives were wiped out in the explosion. Now we have no way of getting him or the four crystals he already has. Nor do we know anything about who has been secretly helping him.

"We also lost the ancient stone tablet. That stupid leader of the Dark Zodiac, ATOSS, destroyed it in a fit of anger. Now we have lost our knowledge of Atlantis and how the boy fits into the recovery of the crystals!"

One of the other aliens interrupted with a thought-question. "Was the time craft we built for them destroyed as well?"

"Yes it was, but no matter. We have the resources to build another," the leader responded.

"But our bodies are still unable to withstand the pressures of time travel." Another alien floating close by reminded them all.

"Then we will have to build a new Dark Zodiac team as well! However, this time we will create more obedient genetic super humans. And construct more powerful robots to help as well," added another.

The leader twisted around with excitement. "It will not be difficult to find another corrupt human Government to help us, in return for our promise of more power for them when we take over the world."

The creature continued, its body pumping in and out like a giant heart. "We may not know the locations of the crystals; however we can still chase the boy if he continues on the quest for the remaining eight crystals. We can still track the TALON when it jumps through time to the next crystal's location."

"So is there a new plan for us to follow, or do we continue to try and get the crystals to use them to take over the world?" challenged another creature. It was not the only alien worried that their previous plan had ended with disaster; when James had destroyed the Dark Zodiac.

The alien leader, who had recently confronted James in the battle with the Dark Zodiac, suddenly swelled and glowed with excitement.

"I have an alternative plan! During the battle I saw how a strange dark rage took control of the boy's personality. I am convinced that it is caused by his exposure to the crystals. I saw him totally consumed with uncontrollable rage. I believe that it would not need much pressure to emotionally tip the boy over the edge to become permanently evil. If that can be done then we could easily persuade the evil side of his personality to get all the crystals for us!"

Collectively all the aliens glowed brightly and exchanged wildly excited thoughts.

As they squirmed, their bodies swelled and their tentacles entwined like a mass of eels.

In the chamber containing the vast tank of liquid, a tunnel door slid open and a group of humans were herded inside. They were chained together and shuffled along slowly, prodded forward by several large metallic humanoid robots. Each captive had a vacant, haunted look on their face, as if they had been hypnotised.

"Food has arrived!" exclaimed one of the aliens, "we must quickly conclude our council of war and stop for a feast!"

The leader pulsated with a bright green glow and separated itself from the rest of the squirming mass.

"Before that we must agree our new strategy!"

Suddenly their mental voices combined into one chorus of chants.

"Track the TALON when it makes its next time burst!

Find the boy and provoke him!

Tip him over the edge!

Turn the boy to evil!

Turn him on to our side!

Make him into one of us!

Use him to get the crystals for us!

Use him to unleash their combined power!

Use him to take over the world for us!"

Chapter 2

"Flaming fireballs, I wanted the crystal quest to be finished!" shouted James, his voice echoing around the cellar (his secret headquarters under his parents' house). Only moments ago he had returned from his revenge-fuelled mission to destroy the headquarters of the Dark Zodiac. Sighing deeply he looked at the four crystals suspended in the *Horoscope Matrix*. The matrix was a constant area of projected energy at the far end of the cellar. The crystals were kept in it; suspended in its energy to float in a slow circular motion.

With the limited resources in the cellar Max had only been able to construct a temporary horoscope matrix; hastily built to prevent the combined energy signatures of the first four crystals from being detected by the Dark Zodiac. It also ensured that the enemy was unable to follow James back to his home above. Unfortunately the enemy had succeeded in tracking James to his home and launched an unsuccessful attack! This was what had sent James into an uncontrollable rage, using the crystals to find and destroy the Dark Zodiac headquarters.

However what James did not know was that Max and Davius had also constructed the matrix to secretly prevent him from gaining access to the collective powers of the crystals. Having seen the ease with which James wielded their power on the last two missions, they had made a secret pact to use the matrix to shield the crystals from *his* influence *as well!* The quest remained the same. James was to get the 12 crystals, then Max was to destroy them to prevent anyone else from using them!

James unclipped TALON from his belt pouch and placed it onto a table top. The (Tracking And Locating Organic

Navigator) was a complex computer the shape and size of a metal cricket ball. However its uncanny ability to know the locations of all the crystals was balanced by its sarcastic electronic voice.

Sitting down on a chair, James stretched and loosened the collar of the time suit. James was reasonably tall for his age and quite thin. His unkempt mop of fair hair hung down in front of his eyes. The material of his alien suit (molecule flexible metal) fitted like a diver's wet suit and had various technical features as well as its time travel abilities.

Max hovered closer to the boy, its round, green, football sized body pulsating slightly. Its single large, unblinking red eye scanned him intensely. Its blotchy skin vibrated at such a fantastic speed it formed sounds which were converted into language. Yet James sometimes wondered if its biological computer brain was also able to read his mind as well!

There were still moments when he did not fully trust the motives of the ugly green computer from a hundred years in the future. Then again he recalled that Max had saved his life on several occasions and had proved itself to be a trusted friend!

Standing opposite was the High Priest Davius. He originally came from Stonehenge and was rescued from the year 302 BC by James. Davius was a tall, grand old man with a long white beard. His long robe was trimmed with strange blue and gold symbols. Despite his long years he was remarkably fit and had saved the boy's life too many times to mention!

James looked wearily at Davius and Max floating next to him.

What a motley bunch! thought James. *These two and TALON were the only friends he had, who knew that he was on this insanely dangerous quest!* Sighing heavily he addressed Max and Davius.

"I did it! I destroyed the aliens, the Dark Zodiac and their secret headquarters. I also regained my senses from the dark influence of the crystals and then returned here successfully."

Davius frowned and Max wobbled with concern, but James continued to blurt out his statements without pausing for breath.

"I have also saved the world. We are alright and my family are safe now as well. I discovered the secrets of the Dark Zodiac and the aliens. The threat from them is over. We have won! The quest is over! There is no more alien threat!"

Max flew closer, about to interrupt James; but the boy carried on talking, his voice getting louder and louder.

"I still have TALON, my suit, and the four crystals I got earlier. You and Davius are now permanently living here in the present period. The Horoscope Matrix is still fully functional."

Having finished his outburst James abruptly stood up and began to pull off his suit. Determined to convince the others, he continued.

"No need for me to go after any more crystals, now the Dark Zodiac is destroyed. With them and the aliens gone, the future where they have succeeded in taking over the world will not happen now. I have succeeded in changing the direction of future events!"

He desperately wanted to go back to being an ordinary school boy. He missed his friends Stephen and Alistair. He hated deceiving them, and even more difficult continually misleading his parents and sister. The pressure of keeping the quest a secret from everyone was putting great pressure on him!

The direct attack by the Dark Zodiac on his family was what had sent him into a crystal-powered rage. His evil side had taken control and he had destroyed them and their secret headquarters. Now it was all over!

Max suddenly flew around the room in near hysterics; sparks leaping out of it.

"How do you know what the future now holds? If the earth is now saved and the aliens have failed, how come I am still here? If the future has changed, their terrible dictatorship would not have been created. Therefore I would not have been constructed by them. In which case I would not have been able to come back to set you on your mission in the first place! If I am still here, then does the Dark Zodiac or their alien masters still triumph in some other way?"

James froze. He had not thought of that. If he had messed things up, then was there a danger that he had created some sort of everlasting time loop!

Max continued, its recently healed skin vibrating wildly. "The whole point of the quest was to get all the crystals first and destroy their collective power, so no one could ever use them for evil. The quest was not about destroying the Dark Zodiac or aliens. By doing that, you may have changed the course of future events for the worse!"

Davius stepped forward, filled with equal concern.

"James, this quest has always been about you getting the crystals first; however it is now obvious that it is *your* unique destiny to get each one. Each time you get one you have had a direct impact on the course of world events. It's now obvious that you are creating history as we know it!"

James sat back down; his head was starting to spin again. He put his head in his hands.

Finally Max calmed down and floated back in front of James.

"Think about it. We now know that you are a *crystal user*. You caused Stonehenge to lose its power and its sacred stones to fall down. It was you who destroyed one of the Ancient Egyptian Sphinx's and also suggested building the Pyramids. It was you who caused the Great Fire of London!"

Stunned, it all suddenly made sense to James. He *had* caused the eruption of Mount Vesuvius and allowed the city of Pompeii to be destroyed.

He was *causing* twelve key historic events to take place. He was creating human history!

He was also being put through twelve tests of his character! He had *allowed* the volcano to explode *knowing* that it would kill so many people. Was it a test to see if he had the strength of will to allow history to take its course; no matter how dreadful the specific events were?

Max pressed him further, sensing that James now realised the enormity of his mission.

"You *must* go and get the other eight crystals; because each time you do you *create* history as we know it! If you don't who knows how badly you will change and damage the course of world events!"

Davius stepped forward to stand in between Max and James.

"Exactly. By refusing to continue the quest and destroying the Dark Zodiac instead, you have lost control of events and may have done more harm than good!"

The old man straightened and sighed heavily.

"There is only one way to settle this, James. You must go into the future and see what happens to the world if you do not continue on the quest!"

Chapter 3

Earlier that day, before James had returned from his victory over the Dark Zodiac, the battle in James's house had ended in victory for Max. However Max had realised that James's parents and sister might notice evidence of the Dark Zodiac attack on the house when they returned. They might then also question where James was and why he had become absent in the last week! Max was determined that the quest remain secret. It did not want his parents interfering and stopping James!

As soon as his family returned home, Max secretly powered-up in the cellar. It narrowed its single eye, and began to vibrate its body very quickly. Suddenly the eye turned yellow and a purple light shone out of it. The purple beam shot straight into the ceiling and passed through without damaging it.

In the house above was James's father Alan – tall, thin, dark-haired, he wore thick black-rimmed spectacles. He was a well known local doctor. James's mother, Christine, was a nurse at the local hospital. She too was tall, but her blonde hair was usually tied up in a pony tail. James's sister Mary was fifteen, with long dark hair, her mother's figure, but a serious attitude problem!

All three had just sat down in the lounge, when the beam rose through the floor and bathed them in the purple light. The beam passed through the floor and furniture without harming it. Suddenly the room was flooded with light and all three slumped back into their seats and fell asleep. The strange light continued to surround them for several minutes and then vanished.

Below, Max stopped vibrating and its eye returned to normal. This was the first time that it had used its *amnesia ray* on living people. It just hoped that it had worked properly. When they woke up in a few hours' time, they would be unaware of what had happened around the house. Now Max could focus all its attention on the quest without distractions. It must make certain that James continued on the quest!

*

In the present, James paced around the cellar deep in thought, while Max and Davius looked on.

"I'll do it! I'll go into the future and see what I have caused to happen. And if I don't like what I see, I'll go back in time to get the stone tablet and read it for myself. I'll see what it actually says about me and my so-called destiny. Whatever I have to do to get this nightmare over with, I will do it!"

Max floated away across the room and then turned back to face James and Davius.

"There is another option. You can take the risk of going back ten thousand years and see what *really* happened to destroy Atlantis. Then take the greatest risk of all and seize the twelve crystals in one go before they are hidden!"

All three remained silent for what seemed minutes as the gravity of the choices and risks dawned on them.

Sitting on the table, TALON muttered to itself. "Flaming fireballs. Just when I thought all this travelling was over, these three clowns are about to throw all of us on the most dangerous missions so far! And I don't know the locations of where we are going this time!"

"And you may need my special powers as well…" finished Davius, pulling his beard thoughtfully.

James sighed again. "So what you are all saying is that we should ALL go into the future; and if needed then go back to ancient Atlantis as well."

The others stayed silent. James paced around for a while, deep in thought. "As long as we are all in physical contact I can time burst us all there, using the power of my alien suit. However I will have no way of protecting us *all* once we arrive there!"

Max rotated to face James. "Do not worry; I can generate an energy bubble to shield and protect us. And TALON can perform all the scanning when we arrive at our destinations."

James sighed even more deeply. He ached all over; suffering from *time fatigue* again. The good night's sleep he had snatched yesterday had eased its ill effects. However prior to that he had not had any proper sleep since he snatched the Egyptian coin containing the coded locations of the crystals, from the local county museum! Since then successive *time bursts* and *location jumps* had added to his fatigue! He now found that he needed a regular energy boost from one of the crystals to keep him going for each mission.

Without consulting either Max or Davius, he reached into the Horoscope Matrix and pulled out the Aquarius crystal. He held the crystal in front of him in both hands, closed his eyes and concentrated. Almost immediately it glowed with a mixture of blue and purple light, and bathed his body in healing energy. After a few moments he felt his body tingling with its invigorating power as it brought him back to full strength.

They watched in silence as he placed the crystal back into the matrix again.

"The crystals must remain here," said Max assertively. "We cannot risk taking them on this mission with us. We dare not lose one, especially if you are going to get the other eight."

James shook his head slightly. "We will see what the future holds. Hopefully I will not have to continue with the quest, if the future looks good."

Max then became even more insistent. "We will go one hundred years into the future but stay at this exact location. That way we will see if the world still turns into a terrible dictatorship run by the Dark Zodiac and aliens."

James nodded and zipped up his suit, then checked his belt pack and wrist controls.

"Let's do it!"

*

The secret alien base was dark and humid. Its organic walls seemed to slowly move as if alive, while bathing the corridors in an eerie green light. In a large chamber, several shadowy shapes with long tentacles writhed and twisted in a big tank of green liquid. As thoughts passed between them, their alien bodies glowed with different colours.

One of the aliens at the centre began to communicate.

"The development of a new set of genetically engineered super humans is well underway. However I doubt if all twelve can be fully developed at once. I had grave reservations about the Dark Zodiac's ability to get the crystals and I doubt if these replacements will be any more successful at stopping the boy."

"I agree," said the leader. "These new ones will remain under our direct control. We will also keep control of the new time craft once it is operational and our existing squads of hunter-killer robots."

"We will be prepared for when the boy makes his next move!" they all thought-exchanged at the same moment.

*

In the cellar the trio were ready to go. James had double checked his time suit and then placed TALON securely into one of the belt pouches. He did not need it to *track* as they were not going to find crystals; but it would be vital for scanning when they arrived at their destination.

Davius stood facing James at arm's length; his lined face pale and serious. Max then floated above them, stopped and hovered down between them. Davius and James extended their arms and held on to the green ball tightly.

"I have set my wrist control to time burst in five seconds time…"

He could feel the strange bond between his skin and his time suit, tingling like pins-and-needles. Suddenly there was an explosion of rainbow-light and all of them vanished in a flash.

*

The time-travel vortex span around James like a kaleidoscope of rainbow colours. He felt as if he was being swept along in a river of warm water. From the moment he had made his first time burst, he had quickly come to enjoy time travel. It was his secret. No other ordinary humans knew how to do it. He found that the few moments he travelled through the vortex, were the most restful he had nowadays. It was a peaceful place-between-worlds, where he could relax from the stresses of the quest. Unfortunately there was a side effect. The more he time travelled the more fatigued he became when he returned from a mission.

Safely suspended in the vortex in front of him were Max and Davius and he could feel TALON vibrating on his belt.

He felt his time suit interacting with his skin. The suit might look flimsy but in fact it was constructed of *molecule-flexible* metal, and harder than steel. The suit also had temperature control sensors, to protect the wearer from extreme climates. It also contained a chemical compound which enabled it to change colour, so it can blend into most backgrounds. The collar contained a collapsible helmet which provided oxygen in emergencies.

Having snatched the alien suit on an earlier mission, he was accidentally baited in the combined energy of the Aquarius crystal, the black gas and liquid of his own crude time travel belt. The energised liquid had soaked through the suit's material and into his skin. This had transferred the mysterious properties of his time travel device into his body and the suit. His skin had now been transformed into the connection between his body and the suit. When he wore it, he was able to travel in time at will. And as it was linked exclusively to his genetic composition, even if someone else wore the suit, they would not be able to use it to travel through time!

Suddenly the warm comfort of the time travel vortex tugged at him and he knew from experience that he was about to land at his destination. However he had yet to perfect a painless landing technique and usually hit the ground on all-fours! He had no idea how the three of them would land!

Chapter 4

The three of them suddenly materialised again; but sooner than James had anticipated. They span off out of control in different directions. Before he could do anything he felt a terrible choking sensation and gasped for air. Luckily his automatic breathing helmet slid up into place to save him; but he knew that Davius would have no way of surviving!

"Hold tight!" boomed Max and it suddenly extended a transparent energy field around them all. To James's astonishment he found himself suspended in mid air and being pulled back towards Max at high speed. At his waist, TALON vibrated wildly and sprang free of its pouch and floated away from James. Within moments TALON, James and Davius were floating next to an agitated Max.

"I can protect us all in this energy bubble, but there is only enough air in here for a few minutes. James will have to *time burst* us back to his house soon," instructed Max with a superior voice.

Taking a deep breath (with his helmet still on), James finally calmed down enough to look around at where they had emerged from their *time burst*. His jaw dropped. This was where his home would be in a hundred years' time. Yet in all directions, as far as the eye could see, there was nothing but a blackened wasteland!

"What happened?" he stammered, still unable to take in the horrific landscape he was looking at.

TALON scanned the area in grim silence; using a wide range of its internal instruments to gather data. Floating next to James it hummed quietly, resisting saying anything which might upset him. Davius was still gathering his wits and taking in great gulps of air, so Max narrowed its big red eye and concentrated on maintaining the bubble. At length TALON stopped its scanning.

"I detect a wide range of radiation pollution and biological poisoning. It extends in all directions as far as I can scan. There are no signs of buildings or living entities. In fact there is noting left at all. Even the hills have been blasted flat and valleys choked with lifeless rubble. Only this flattened, charred landscape exists…."

James sank to his knees and put his head in his hands. "What have I done? By destroying the Dark Zodiac and refusing to continue with the crystal quest, I have changed the course of future events. Instead of saving the world I have destroyed it!"

Davius bent down next to him and put his arms on his young shoulders. "This confirms what we feared. You have to get all the crystals, if the future earth is to be saved."

Max rotated around to face them both. "Exactly as I said! You still have to get them one at a time in the correct order!"

James stood up and shook his head in defiance. "No! I will not put myself through another eight deadly missions! Each time I go after one I put my life on the line!"

"But you have no choice…" retorted Max.

"What does Master James have in mind?" interjected TALON, hoping to stop the growing argument.

The boy stiffened and looked at the desolation around him; determined to make sure that the world was not destroyed because of his failure to get the crystals.

"The next step is to go back ten thousand years to Atlantis and get all the crystals in one go!"

TALON suddenly hummed and chattered with nervous excitement. "The action never stops…!" it snapped sarcastically at all three of them.

Davius looked from James to Max. "It will be dangerous to get all crystals in one go. If you do that you are still failing to set in motion twelve key historic events. Also remember what the ancient stone tablet warned of. It is your destiny to get them one at a time!" warned Max.

Davius tried to find common ground between the boy and Max. "The man-child may be right. Perhaps it is time to go back to ancient Atlantis and discover why it exploded. Perhaps we should at least know why all the crystals were hidden and James has to get them?"

Max rotated slowly several times, deep in thought. "We must take the risk. The stakes are too great not to. This quest becomes more complicated with every twist and turn!"

TALON muttered to itself. The quest had been so straight forward when it started. Its computerised role had been clear; to give the locations of the crystals to James one at a time in strict order. Now all that was being cast aside! Angry and confused it kept its views to itself and just muttered under its electronic breath.

With a determined look etched onto his face, James concentrated on his wrist control and punched in the co-ordinates for ancient Atlantis. The time period was not too difficult, as Max already had an accurate date; but where was it located?

Davius leant towards him. "Ancient British legends tell that it was a large Island in the north Atlantic, several days sailing south west from what is now Cornwall."

"I can protect us with this energy bubble if we materialise slightly off course," added Max confidently. "And I can scan for the island, when we get to the time period," finished TALON.

Nodding with satisfaction, James completed entering the co-ordinates into his wrist device and pushed the main control button. As before, he had entered a five-second delay, so he and Davius quickly put their hands on Max to make the connection complete. Suddenly there was a rainbow flash of swirling light and they all disappeared.

Chapter 5

Whirling through the time vortex again, Davius felt sick. This was completely different from the type of ghostly astral-projections which he was able to make when he was living in ancient Stonehenge. Events were moving at an ever increasing pace. One minute he was living in his own time period, the next James had saved his life and brought him to live in the present period.

During his long life the High Priest had developed many ways in which he could see into the past and future. James had told him that there was always a scientific explanation for the things the High Priest could do, no matter how magical they seemed. For his part Davius did not care how he was able to tap into the incredible forces; he was just glad that he could.

Since giving the Aquarius crystal to James, the High Priest's powers had become limited. As he was no longer the keeper of the Aquarius crystal, life had become more difficult. Stonehenge was still the centre of the ancient Britons' faith but since the Dark Scorpio had damaged it during the battle with James, its powers had begun to wane. Yet he had still managed to project himself across time to save the boy's life on several occasions (Ancient Egypt, the fire of London and the destruction of Pompeii). He had also been able to rescue James from the negative influence of the crystals on one occasion.

Suddenly the warm comfort of the time travel vortex tugged at him and he knew from his last experience that he was about to land at the next destination. He just hoped that Max was better prepared with his energy bubble this time. He almost suffocated last time!

*

The alien's mystery base was bathed in eerie green light which ebbed and flowed from the organic looking brown walls. The sound of flowing liquid reverberated throughout the strange structure like a moaning voice. The massive chamber was brimming with transparent green ooze in which the large jelly fish-like aliens swam.

The largest one suddenly glowed a deep purple and went motionless, its thoughts being transmitted to its colleagues close by.

"I have just received a communication from the scanning control centre. They are detecting some unusual energy patterns. It could be that TALON is moving through time. However it does not appear to be using its own in-built tracking abilities, our scanners are unable to pinpoint to which time period it has travelled."

One of the other creatures glowed a pale yellow in response. "This is yet another setback. I thought that we would be able to track the TALON?"

"I agree!" thought a third creature, "how will we be able to get at the boy otherwise?"

"Contact has been lost," responded the first creature, pulsating and thrashing about with its tentacles. "However we have nothing to fear. Whatever the boy and TALON are doing, they have not gone to get another crystal. If they had, then TALON would have to use its abilities and we would know exactly where they had gone! The longer they leave it to get the next crystal, the longer we have to complete the new time craft. Time, as the humans so quaintly put it, *is on our side!*"

*

They all tumbled out of mid air, but this time safely contained within the energy bubble generated by Max. After a few moments they all stopped spinning and settled into upright positions. Looking around, James saw that they were floating

19

several hundred metres above the ocean. Unfortunately there was no sign of land.

"Are we in the wrong time period or the wrong location?" grumbled James with a heavy, questioning sigh.

From his waist TALON chattered a response. "Both, you dimwit! We need to go back another twenty-one years and re-appear a hundred and fifty kilometres further south west."

Sensing the boy's frustration it quickly added, "But not bad considering you had ten thousand years and the entire North Atlantic Ocean to choose from!"

Davius nodded in support, but was more concerned with combating his growing sense of travel sickness. Meanwhile Max had narrowed its eye because of extreme concentration, in order to maintain the protective energy bubble. It would only be able to maintain the bubble for a short while longer.

Taking TALON's advice, James completed entering the co-ordinates into his wrist device and pushed the main control button. Once again there was a rainbow flash of swirling light and they all disappeared.

*

An instant later they reappeared in mid air over a vast city. The energy bubble shuddered like wobbling jelly and they all fell onto its firm, but stretchy floor.

"What's wrong!" exclaimed James, getting to his feet.

Max closed its big red eye with the sheer effort of concentration. "The city below is in turmoil. There are unpredictable energy spikes erupting all over the place. We won't be able to stay here for very long."

James looked down at the sprawling city. It was a marvel of engineering, huge buildings and ornate structures extended in all directions. Many seemed to be constructed out of crystal and precious metals. Indeed it looked as if some buildings had grown out of the ground like living crystals, designed to specific order.

However he also noticed that fires were breaking out all over the city. In the distance, where James could see what he thought was a huge sea port, the area was suddenly rocked by a series of explosions. The bright flashes of the eruptions reflected on the distant sea.

"I detect fighting, Master James..." chattered TALON. "Warfare is spreading across the island and engulfing the city."

"I can only maintain this bubble for so much longer..." cautioned Max, "Plus I now have to use extra power to shield us from the city's detection equipment. I will only be able to keep us invisible for a short stay here..."

James unclipped TALON from his belt and held it up in front of his face. "Can you detect the crystals, TALON?"

The metal ball hummed and clicked for a moment. "Yes, Master, the energy they are radiating is so strong that I cannot miss them!"

Following TALON's directions, the bubble with them all inside swooped down towards a huge temple-like building, made of crystals and jewels. It had massive arched openings spiralling up the main tower, and their bubble was able to fly inside the building unseen.

Once inside, Max guided the bubble silently through the large deserted corridors. It was as if the building had been evacuated in great haste, as all sorts of personal items had been left scattered everywhere. Davius and James marvelled at the intricate designs on the walls and ceilings. This was clearly a place of great knowledge and architecture. "Some of these symbols are familiar to me," muttered the old man. "The language of the ancient Britons obviously descended from Atlantis."

Suddenly the bubble darted to the left and they entered a large glowing chamber. Despite the protection of the bubble, James could feel the energy within the room causing the hairs on his head to stand on end. He looked at Davius and saw the ridiculous sight of the old man's long beard and hair all pointing upwards as if he had just had an electric shock!

Abruptly the bubble stopped and hovered silently.

Below them there were two figures. One was an old man and the other was a boy. Surrounding them were the twelve crystals! James peered down closely through narrow eyes. He could feel the crystals' power calling to him like twelve whispering voices in his head. Each twinkled and glowed with a different colour, creating a constantly changing rainbow of light around the two figures below. It was as if the crystals were creating a hypnotic rhythm, calling James to jump down and take them. They were each set into sockets in a circular metal control table. The centre of the table was hollow and the two figures stood in it. The man was totally occupied with the controls in front of him. It was a super-sized Horoscope matrix! Suddenly the old man stopped what he was doing and looked up at them!

James froze. For a moment he feared that they had been discovered, however after a moment the man looked away. Perhaps he could sense the presence of the invisible spies but he could not see them.

But what shocked James even more was that the man looked identical to Davius!

*

By now James's parents and sister were up and getting ready to go out. The amnesia ray which Max had bathed them in earlier had done its job well. None of them could remember any of the previous attack.

Things were back to normal. Mother looked Mary up and down in despair. She wore a skirt too short, a T-shirt advertising an unpronounceable boy band and big boots a builder might wear. But at least she wasn't wearing the multiple ear rings and black lipstick this time, sighed her mother with relief. She also hoped that the big argument the three of them had recently about Mary's secret drinking and smoking had put a stop to the bad behaviour.

But in her head Mary was miles away. She had a strange nagging doubt about what James was involved in. Despite not being able to remember anything of the previous day, she still had strange images of James in her head.

She was convinced he was up to something and she wanted to get to the bottom of her horrid little brother's mystery!

Chapter 6

James gaped down at the old man in the centre of the massive Horoscope Matrix. His clothes were completely different to those worn by Davius, but other than that he looked identical to the High Priest!

Davius had also spotted what the man looked like, and stood with his mouth wide open, eyes transfixed on the figure below. He was totally stunned.

"How do you explain this?" said James tentatively, utterly confused. Max remained silent, concentrating on keeping the bubble invisible; while TALON continued to scan as far as it could in all directions, in case the explosions outside were getting nearer.

Davius slumped into a sitting position on the slightly bouncy floor of the energy bubble; his hair still standing ridiculously upright.

"I cannot explain this. I do not understand!"

James sighed; Davius was not usually lost for words. "There must be some explanation Davius…"

Recovering from the shock, the High Priest stood up and stroked his beard as he thought. "There is one explanation. It was believed that the family line of my ancient British tribe originally came from Atlantis. It could never be proved, but this confirms it. My long lost ancestors were high priests in ancient Atlantis!"

James shrugged his shoulders in confusion. "It would explain how your family line came to be the protectors of the Aquarius crystal. It must have been taken from here and hidden where Stonehenge would eventually be built. It also explains how you were handed down the ancient prophecy about me."

Davius lent against the wall of the bubble and nodded slightly. "That would seem to make sense."

Standing next to each other they both peered down at the two figures as they operated various instruments on the fantastic-looking equipment. Around them the crystals pulsated faster and faster. At the back of his mind James could hear them still whispering to him. Enticing him to snatch them for himself! He shook his head to banish the temptation.

Staring down again he saw the boy turn away from the Davius look-a-like and check a different set of instruments. Suddenly the boy turned in the opposite direction and James gasped as he saw that the boy looked just like him!

*

The aliens had left the comfort and security of the liquid-filled chamber and were travelling through the base. Each was a hideous creature with long, writhing tentacles and was surrounded by a solid transparent bubble, like a huge goldfish bowl. In this, their liquid-filled transport sphere, they floated through the twisting tunnels of the base.

"The first of the new hunter-killer robots is completed," the leader boomed in an artificial voice which echoed through the corridors. The alien did not have a mouth, or any noticeable features, except its unpleasant, translucent skin. However it liked to use its ability to translate its telepathy into audible sounds from time to time. This gave it a sense of power, not having to rely solely on thought transference all the time.

The main laboratory was bathed in an eerie green light which ebbed and flowed from the organic walls. It was a strange room. It was a contrast of organic walls and the hard technical equipment it contained. On all sides the walls were lined with dozens of metallic frames, each holding up a humanoid-shaped robot. Each robot was a complicated structure formed of a shiny skeleton and complex mass of

25

cables. Its head was an enclosed metal skull with a single red eye.

Each unblinking eye scanned the world around it.

The leading alien floated towards the nearest frame and sent a telepathic command to the robot it contained. Suddenly the metallic creation jerked as if jolted with electricity and its red eye glowed into life.

The alien squirmed with excitement in its protective transparent sphere. "The first robot is now fully programmed to go after the boy. Now all we have to do is complete preparations on the time craft…"

*

James gasped. He was looking at an identical twin! The boy below had his face. His haircut was different and his clothes were strange, but otherwise he was the same size and shape.

"I hope that's not me out there and in here at the same time on a different mission; caused by some weird twist of time travel?" groaned James out loud.

"No," said Davius shaking his head. "That must be one of your ancestors as well! Remember what I said about the ancient Britons' prophecies when we first met. And remember what Max told you when he first contacted you. It is your *destiny* to go on this quest. It's now become clear why. Your ancestors were the original owners of the crystals!"

James felt faint and slumped to the floor of the bubble. Over the years the family name of *light-water* must have evolved to hide the secret.

Suddenly he was rudely shaken from his confused thoughts by a loud explosion!

"The fighting outside has reached this building!" alerted TALON anxiously.

*

The sound of flowing liquid reverberated throughout the strange alien base, causing the structure to moan like a fierce animal's roar. The solid looking walls seemed to respond in some unnatural way, expanding and contracting as if breathing.

Several of the aliens floated down a spiralling network of tunnels, each man-sized jelly fish deliberately stretching its long, writhing tentacles as they travelled in their transparent bubbles.

"The time craft is almost complete!" exclaimed the leading alien as they entered a low-ceiling chamber.

In the centre of the dimly lit chamber hovered a motionless craft, which resembled a car-sized flying saucer. Except that it was transparent, like a ghost-ship!

The alien time travel device was a *virtual-machine* and could follow wherever the TALON guided James, surrounding itself with a time-warp distortion. The alien machine existed in an alternative reality but could be physically materialised in our world. Once used, it de-materialised and returned to its alternative reality until it was needed again. The user controlled it by means of a tiny homing beacon. The user would swallow the beacon and while it remained inside them, they could summon the craft to their location at any time.

"Just a few more re-calibration tests and it will be ready for the robot to use!" the leader proclaimed proudly with a loud booming voice.

Chapter 7

The power of James's time suit was straining to hold them all in the volatile time period. Max also fought hard to maintain the energy bubble they floated in and TALON extended its scanning range as far as possible.

Below, the boy and man continued with their frantic work. The closeness of the explosion outside the building had clearly spurred them on. Carefully Max lowered the bubble so that they could all hear the conversation between the boy and man.

The old man continued working on the glowing controls while he spoke to the boy who was busy operating similar instruments.

"We have to hide all twelve crystals before they can be captured. If they fall into the wrong hands they could be used for terrible evil!" he exclaimed.

"Should we activate the time disperser now, Master?" responded the boy looking up at him.

Another explosion rocked the building causing small pieces of debris to fall to the floor at the far side of the chamber.

The man nodded in response to the younger one and pressed a large glowing red button on the control panel in front of him.

In response, a panel opened in the glass-like floor in front of them and a spinning object floated out of it. Gradually spinning faster it rose high into the vaulted chamber and suddenly stopped.

In the hidden bubble James looked at it closely. It resembled a glass sphere twice the size of a football. Inside it he saw a strangely coloured angular rock, around which swirled dark smoke.

Once again his mouth dropped open with astonishment. "It's just like one of the mysterious fossils I found on holiday last year! The ones with the strange black gas which triggered the black hole in my bedroom. The one which Max came through! That glass sphere around it must be their version of my everlasting light bulb!"

Even as he gasped, the spinning object suddenly expelled a kaleidoscope of rainbow colour throughout the huge chamber. Max groaned as the incredible power it was creating buffeted the energy sphere they were hidden inside.

Before any of them could say a word, a large twisting black hole opened in the air beneath the spinning glass sphere. Just like the one which had opened in James's bedroom at the start of the quest!

On the floor, the old man continued to touch his glowing controls and talk to the boy.

"The time disperser will allow us to hide all the crystals at once. It will send each one to a different location and time period in a specific order. A deliberate order which will step by step trigger key events for this planet. Twelve key events which will culminate in a thirteenth cataclysmic battle for the survival of the world."

Looking up they saw the black hole twisting and quivering like a living thing; it was beginning to pull at the surrounding building, threatening to suck in anything which was not fixed down.

In the invisible energy sphere, Max fought to stop them being sucked into the hole themselves!

Suddenly twelve tentacles of living lightning shot out of the black hole and one striking each crystal. All at once the glowing, twisting lightning snatched up the crystals and pulled them into the black hole! As they vanished inside, the chamber was filled with an incredible beast-like howl and a gust of icy wind.

Max's invisible energy bubble span towards the black hole out of control, throwing James and Davius onto its wobbly floor. "We'll get ripped apart if we go in there!" he exclaimed, his hand reaching towards his wrist controls, ready to *time burst* the four of them away from Atlantis!

Suddenly the spinning glass sphere stopped firing out its rainbow light and the black hole shrank to the size of a football. Shuddering, Max regained control of the energy bubble and floated it back towards the two people on the ground.

The man continued to operate the controls and talk to the boy at the same time.

"One day, young man, one of your descendants will have the task of finding all the crystals in the correct order. He will have to do this to trigger specific historic events, which will lead the human race to a final climatic battle for the survival of the planet ten thousand years from now!"

"How will he know where to get the crystals, this descendant of mine ten thousand years from now?" responded the boy.

"The final battle has two possible outcomes. I cannot control whether good or evil prevails. However I can ensure that each crystal can only be found at specific moments in time; thereby engineering the course of history."

He opened a carry case which was sat on the console next to him. Out of it he pulled two things – a gold coin and a stone tablet the size of an A4 sheet of paper.

"On the coin I have etched the coded locations of the crystals. One day, when the technology is right someone will create a device which can read the directions."

Hovering within listening distance again, James gasped and gripped Davius for support. He was the descendant! It really WAS his destiny to get the crystals. The coin the man was holding was the coin now inserted inside TALON! For a moment in time it was in two places at once!

Below, the man waved the stone tablet. "On this I have set out in code the twelve missions your descendants must complete in the quest to get the crystals. The historic events ARE set in stone; however the final battle IS NOT set in stone.

The outcome will depend on how brave, honest and determined your descendant is!"

"What happens to the coin and tablet?" questioned the boy; anxious to complete their task, as another explosion rumbled outside. There were only minutes left before the enemy would burst into the building.

"The coin and tablet are going to our colony in Egypt. While you and I will flee to the British peninsular with the last of the black-gas fossils. We will hide them there for your descendant to find ten thousand years from now. Then we will establish a dynasty of High Priests to keep alive the legend of Atlantis and memory of the crystals."

"What if the enemy follows us through the time disperser, Master?" said the boy.

"I have set everything to self-destruct as soon as we leave here. The resulting explosion will create a chain reaction which will destroy the city and sink the island! The explosion will cause a huge rise in water levels and shift in the warm water patterns of the Atlantic Ocean. The floods will cause the British peninsular to be separated from the continent. The British peninsular will then become a sacred isle of its own; ready for us the keep alive the memories of Atlantis in the teachings of the ancient Britons."

Pressing the large red control again, he threw the coin and tablet into the air. Two lightning-bolt tentacles lashed out of the black hole, caught them in mid air and pulled them into it.

As this happened the boy lifted up two back-packs, each filled with the mysterious fossils containing the black gas.

"Are you ready?" said the old man with a reassuring smile.

"I am, Master."

Without another word the old man pressed the red control again and they stood motionless. High above them the black hole suddenly grew larger again and two lightning-tentacles snaked down towards them! In an instant they were engulfed in white light and pulled up into the hole.

James and Davius looked on in awe; their mysterious ancestors had vanished, setting ten thousand years of destiny in motion!

Suddenly the controls below began to explode and spit flames in all directions. Great cracks began to race up the walls of the building, collapsing pieces of crystal masonry into the chamber.

"Time to get out of here!" shouted James at the top of his voice.

"Home, James!" snapped TALON sarcastically.

With a touch of his controls the energy bubble and its four occupants vanished in a flash of rainbow light; to jump forward to their own time period.

*

The seven alien jelly fish, each surrounded by a solid transparent bubble, had assembled in the main control area.

On the far wall, there was a large window where they could observe the life support chamber. The massive chamber was brimming with transparent green ooze in which a few other large jelly fish-like aliens swam.

The leading alien guided his transparent travel sphere in to the centre of the circle of aliens.

"We have just detected another flicker of distortion in the time vortex. The TALON and the boy are on the move again. But because they are not using TALON to locate crystals we are unable to get a firm fix on where they are coming from or going to. We can only make a rough calculation that they are returning to the present period."

Another alien glowed with excitement. "Our time craft is now operational and ready for use. The robot is being put into it at this very moment. As it is a robot it cannot swallow the tiny homing beacon, so it is being inserted into the robot's chest plate, ready for activation."

"Good, good," thought the leader, using its telepathy to communicate to them all at once.

"Our *virtual time-travel craft will* follow wherever the TALON guides James. I have every confidence that the boy will go after another crystal soon! And then we will have him!"

This time the sound of flowing liquid reverberated throughout the strange structure like haunting laughter and the walls seemed to vibrate in response.

Chapter 8

Whirling through the time vortex again, Max felt disorientated. It had not been designed to undertake such journeys. Nor was it able to maintain the energy bubble any longer. It just hoped that James kept a tight grip on it! It was a master computer with tremendous electronic abilities and defence mechanisms; but it was ill equipped to undertake repeated time bursts.

One minute it was living in its own secret location, the next it had got James to save its life and bring it to live in the cellar.

Once there Max had swiftly put its abilities to use. Floating from room to room it had converted the boy's father's cellar into a new headquarters. It had been difficult to link into the gas, water, electric and telecommunications networks without the authorities discovering. But the ugly green computer had done it! It had even managed to make the cellar more habitable for James by installing a makeshift air circulation system. Most of this had been achieved by levitating into position equipment left by the boy, or magnetically manipulating the utilities of the house above.

Now that the initial work had been completed, it needed to focus on the most important task – building a permanent Horoscope Matrix to hold all twelve crystals.

The existing one it had made was only temporary; hastily built to prevent the combined energy signatures of the first crystals from being detected by the Dark Zodiac and aliens.

Suddenly the time travel vortex tugged at it, distorting it slightly into the shape of a large rugby ball! It knew from its last experience that they were about to land at their next destination. It just hoped that without the energy bubble they would not have a bad landing!

They all emerged out of the time vortex a metre in the air and fell headlong in different directions onto the dusty cellar floor.

Shaking his head, James sat up and dusted himself off. Davius groaned loudly and stretched his left arm out; he had landed awkwardly on his left shoulder. At least he would be able to use one of the crystals to heal the damage, thought James.

Max had bounced onto the floor and rolled out of control until it thudded into the far wall. Rotating on the floor, it turned to face him and narrowed its single red eye. However it did not make any attempt to fly. Maintaining the protective bubble had drained its power cells. It would need time to recharge itself.

TALON had popped out of the boy's hand and clattered across the floor to hit one of the work benches with a loud clang. "Dimwit!" it exclaimed in annoyance.

James turned and faced Davius, trusting the old man's judgment better than anyone's.

"We just saw Atlantis explode and sink didn't we?" he said with an air of disbelief in his young voice.

The High Priest pulled back his hair with his uninjured hand and nodded. "Yes and what is more, young man, we have seen the future and what happens to the world if you do not get all the crystals one at a time, in strict order."

James nodded slowly. "I know, I know... it's my destiny. My ancestors *and yours* lumbered me with it! But what caused Atlantis to explode?" mused James out loud.

Finally Max had re-charged itself enough to vibrate again and speak.

"The last ice age began about 110,000 BC and reached its zenith about 12,000 BC. The ice sheets extended over large areas of the world. But then the ice which had taken hundreds of thousands of years to build up, suddenly melted in a terrifying thaw. This triggered off natural disasters which were almost catastrophic. All over the world the fossil records indicate an extinction event on a massive scale. In particular the period between 11,000 BC and 8,000 BC was characterised by sustained flooding and worldwide devastation. There are many mountain-top mass graves all over the world, showing the migration of terrified animals and people from the rising flood water. During this period the area of land forming the British peninsular flooded and became separated from Europe to form into the modern day British Isles."

James thought for a moment. "So the sinking of Atlantis caused the world to flood, creating the oceans as they are today. Also the gulf stream of warm water was unblocked and came across the north Atlantic, ending the ice age in Europe and creating the British Isles."

"And some of the survivors of Atlantis came to the British Isles to settle, and create the mystic dynasty my ancestors come from," added Davius.

The three of them sat in silence for a moment, taking in the enormity of the revelation.

"Oi you lot! So much for history lessons. Are we going to get any more crystals or not?" shouted TALON loudly, breaking the silence. "I am getting decidedly fed up sitting on this grubby floor waiting for you three to stop chatting and get on with it!"

Dumbstruck all three simply looked at the tiny metal ball.

*

Having established that his parents and sister had gone out, James location jumped up into the house to use the toilet, have a shower and get some food and drink from the kitchen. He also needed a few hours to wind down from the ordeals of the recent missions. However while he was away Davius and Max held a secret conversation.

Having regained its hovering power, Max floated across the cellar and came to a halt in front Davius; intent on expressing its concerns.

"The boy lost control when he got the last crystal and went on his rash, headstrong attack on the Dark Zodiac headquarters. For a short while his rage unleashed his darker side. He may have returned to normal now, but who knows what could trigger him to unleash his dark side again..."

Davius nodded in agreement. "The whole purpose of the Horoscope Matrix was to shield the energy signatures of the crystals from the aliens, but also to secretly prevent James from harnessing their power for himself!"

With a deep sigh he began to pace around the cellar. "There is no way of knowing if using the crystals in his recent state of anger has permanently affected his mind."

Max wobbled with frustration and span around several times, like a spinning top.

Davius placed a hand on the wobbling sphere to calm it down.

"He is a boy, with all the emotions and instincts you would expect from someone his age. Between us we must help, guide and watch him."

Max narrowed its big red eye, "Especially watch him..."

Chapter 9

"In your absence I have made a few enhancements to TALON," announced Max proudly once James had location jumped back down into the cellar.

Without waiting for the boy to put the bag of supplies onto the floor, it turned to face TALON which was positioned on a workbench.

"Watch."

Taking its cue, TALON began to vibrate very fast and make a high-pitched whine.

"I know about its sonic defence systems," sniffed James unimpressed.

"But not this!" retorted Max.

TALON vibrated even faster and suddenly began to wobble. For a moment it looked as if the little metal ball was going to fall onto the floor, instead it rolled over the edge and stopped in mid air!

"It can fly!" exclaimed the boy with disbelief.

"Not quite," interrupted Max, "but it can hover at low heights for short periods, by vibrating its armoured shell at a particular level. A new level which I have calibrated into its mechanisms."

"Cool," nodded James approvingly.

"Hopefully this will stop you dropping me all over the place!" sniggered TALON in its electronic voice, before hovering back over to the work bench and landing.

"Any chance of cutting a fly onto my time suit before I time burst again?" enquired James back to Max. "I'm fed up with having to pull it all the way down to my knees before I can go to the toilet!"

Max rotated and stared at the boy; dumbfounded that such a minor thing was so important to him.

"The boy has a point. It must be very uncomfortable in that suit, without the added problem of needing the toilet!" added Davius, realising that machines such as Max and TALON would have no understanding of James's predicament.

Max floated towards James and narrowed its eye. "Very well; take off the suit and I will insert a self-sealing fly in it. You can be mission-briefed by TALON while I am making it."

Without hesitation James eagerly slipped the suit off and laid it out flat on the floor. Max floated over it and rotated its eye under its body to face downwards. Suddenly a fine red laser beam the width of a hair shot down and Max began to cut a perfectly positioned fly into the suit.

Meanwhile James was by the bench with TALON on, putting items into his back pack.

"Master James is to get the Leo Crystal next. It is one of the fire sign crystals and is made of Sapphire. It should be angular in shape and fist sized. After diamond, it is the second hardest mineral known to man. You got a Diamond on your last mission for the Aries crystal. Unfortunately I am not clear what the Leo crystal's powers are, but it is supposed to provide strength and aid victory. However my sensors should easily locate it when we get there. It should be a clear blue and hexagonal."

James nodded in silent understanding as he finished checking his equipment. While he knew that he had destroyed the aliens and Dark Zodiac, he also knew that each crystal still had a guardian. Each guardian had powers to protect it, and not all those he had met so far had been prepared to give up the crystals willingly!

"Where and what period are we going to get this crystal from, TALON?"

"Master, the sequence instructs that we will have to go to 1 August 1588. The location is Kent in England. Dover castle to be exact."

James remembered his history lessons at school. "The Spanish Armada! King Philip II of Spain tried to invade England but failed. England was led by Queen Elizabeth I."

"Well done, Master!" encouraged TALON.

"Your suit is ready," interrupted Max, "The fly opening is complete and will self-seal after each use."

Without hesitation James eagerly pulled the suit back on and Max floated over to the Horoscope Matrix.

"You will have to go on this mission without taking any of the four crystals we already have."

James was only half listening as he tested the fly in the suit several times by opening and closing it. It was funny how small things fascinated some humans, thought TALON.

"I know; it's too dangerous to risk losing the crystals," answered James.

"I will go with you instead," added Max.

Finishing strapping on his belt and electrical equipment, James looked up at max and nodded. "OK, if you feel that it's necessary."

"Then I will remain here," added Davius still exhausted.

"Just strap me to your belt and we can go," concluded TALON.

Without another sound being uttered, James picked up TALON and clipped it to his belt. Meanwhile Max floated over and hovered directly in front of the boy's face.

James punched the co-ordinates into his wrist control and then reached out with his hand and grasped Max.

Suddenly there was a blinding flash and a swirling vortex of rainbow light appeared in the cellar. A moment later and they vanished, leaving Davius alone in the cellar.

*

"The TALON and boy have made a time burst!" exclaimed the chief alien with delight. "Our equipment is tracking their progress…"

"Launch the time craft. Send it after them!" urged the other aliens, as they span around in their self-contained floating spheres.

"Do not worry, the time travel craft is a *virtual-machine* and can follow wherever the TALON guides the boy," replied the leader, shining with a confident gold glow. "The on-board robot has the tiny homing beacon inserted inside it. It is ready to go after them."

Elsewhere in the alien base hovered a motionless transparent craft, which resembled a car-sized flying saucer. Inside the sealed craft sat the humanoid-shaped robot; its head an enclosed metal skull with a single red eye. Its body was a complicated structure of shiny skeleton and complex mass of cables.

Suddenly it jerked into life and operated the crafts controls as it identified TALON's destination. The craft glowed with brilliant light and then vanished without a sound.

Chapter 10

James's sister, Mary, returned from the shops in frustration and paced around her bedroom feeling angry and flustered. She still wore her very short skirt, a T-shirt and builder's boots; just to spite her parents. She was almost sixteen; and could do what she wanted!

However, knowing that her mother would shout at her again, she had decided to restrict her secret drinking and smoking to when she was away from the house, with her friends. No one, especially her mother and father, were going to put a stop to her bad behaviour!

James's mum and dad may have woken up with no memory of what had happened when they had been attacked by the Dark Zodiac; however Mary had remained in a confused state. The amnesia ray which Max had bathed her parents with earlier had done its job well, however her mind was still racing and filled with vivid images. The same images she had seen while twisting back and forth as she had slept. She had seen her brother in her nightmares! Seen him surrounded by terrible monsters and explosions of lava and fire!

She could sense that her horrid little brother was up to no good. Angry and frustrated she plonked herself down onto her bed heavily and caused one of its springs to ping!

She was so worked up, that she had to do something about the strange nagging doubts she had about him.

While everyone was out she would sneak into his bedroom and see what she could find!

*

Whirling through the time vortex again, James felt disorientated this time. He still thought that humans (especially boys like him) had not been designed to undertake such journeys. Opening his eyes he saw that they were surrounded by the rainbow of swirling light. In front of him he held tightly on to Max. He knew that it was a master computer with tremendous electronic abilities, but was it equipped to undertake repeated time bursts?

In the short time remaining before they arrived at their destination, James recalled how the quest had started and what he knew about Max…

When Maximus-Prime had first burst through the time door into James's bedroom it had told him many things. So many that the boy's head had spun with fear, confusion and excitement!

The first thing Max had said was that it was a highly complex living computer from a hundred years in the future. A future where the world is controlled by a World Government run by a secret society of genetically engineered, super-humans, manipulated by their secret alien masters.

However Max had said that it and a small band of freedom fighters had rebelled and gone deep underground to start a resistance movement against them.

And then without warning Max had been sucked back into James's time period by the time door opened by the boy's everlasting light bulb experiment!

Max explained there was one week until the Dark Zodiac would begin the quest for the 12 crystals which would give them the power to take over the world and let the aliens secretly steal away thousands of people for food.

Max warned that the leader of the Dark Zodiac had already discovered information about the 12 crystals, time travel and done a terrible deal with secretive alien beings.

Their leader had discovered a secret ancient stone tablet in the vaults of the British museum. The tablet explained about the ancient island of Atlantis and the zodiac crystals being hidden. (Now James had seen with his own eyes what had happened. And he was lumbered with completing the quest by his and Davius's ancestors.)

Max also explained about the code on the Egyptian coin which revealed the exact location of each crystal. As soon as the Dark Zodiac had the locations they then used the alien time machine to go and get the crystals in the correct order.

Once they had them, they unleashed their combined power on the unsuspecting world, and audaciously tricked everyone into voting for the creation of a single World Government, which abolished democracy and set up processing camps.

Most frightening, Max warned that if James allowed events to follow their existing course, then he and his family would be among the first of those rounded up and shipped off to one of the alien *processing* camps.

Max had told him that it was his destiny to go on the quest, because he was an Aquarian, the chosen birth sign of the zodiac. His name *Light - water*, translates directly into "*light as air*" and water is *water*. Aquarius is an *air sign* and is known as the *"water carrier"*. (Now James knew how his ancestors had been given the name.)

More over it was no coincidence that the coin containing the crystals' locations was in his local museum. It was thousands of years old yet it had found its way close to him! Not only this but Max cautioned him that the ancient stone tablet in the British museum, stated that someone from the Aquarius star sign will open a time door and travel through time to save the world. (Now James had seen the tablet for himself!)

Once persuaded to go on the mission, James had quickly developed his time suit and once he had the coin, he inserted it into TALON and it guided him to the first crystals.

Suddenly James felt the familiar tug of the time vortex as he was about to arrive at his destination. Gripping Max tightly he closed his eyes and braced himself for the usual undignified impact!

Chapter 11

"Are you alright, Master James and Master Maximus-Prime?" enquired TALON from its position strapped to James's belt. The small metal sphere thought that it was important to check on their welfare in addition to tracking the crystals.

The three of them had emerged from the time-jump in one piece; with James managing to land comfortably on both feet!

"TALON, do something useful for a change and scan the area to see if we have been followed through the time vortex," he snapped back.

James had learned the hard way on previous missions that his pursuers could track TALON whenever it jumped through time. He needed to know straight away if the enemy had followed him!

Suddenly he cancelled his order to TALON. "Don't bother. Since I destroyed the aliens and the Dark Zodiac in their secret underground base, there is no longer anyone left to follow us!"

James let go of Max and looked around them to see where they had landed. Max floated free for a second but fell to the floor with a load smack.

"Are you alright, Max?" whispered the boy, conscious not to make too much noise until he had established where they were.

"I will be alright in a minute. Time travel affects me badly. I will have to re-boot myself and power up again."

While the green ball went about its complicated re-start process, James took the opportunity to look around them. It was night time and only a few distant flickering torches illuminated the darkness.

They were on the top of a sizable battlement, set on a castle rampart. "Dover castle!" whispered the boy.

TALON hummed excitedly. "Master, this part of the castle seems to be isolated from the rest. We are alone up here on this section and cannot be overseen by anyone."

"Strange. No one could possibly know that we were coming; I wonder what is going on?" the boy thought out loud.

"Master I detect the Leo crystal. I now have a clear and strong signal," whirred the small tracker on his belt.

"Even stranger," said James, "We usually have to waste a lot of time tracking each one down!"

TALON suddenly whirred and vibrated even more. "Master, the crystal is in the castle below us and what is more it is moving towards us!"

"Max, what do you make of this?" the boy whispered.

The green ball swivelled around on the floor and widened its big red eye. "I am unable to compute at the moment. My re-boot process will take a few more minutes."

Suddenly a trapdoor opened in the floor a few metres away from them and light flooded upwards out of it.

Not knowing what was going on, James decided that they should hide until the situation became clearer. Stooping down, he snatched up Max with both hands and dived for cover behind a stack of wooden barrels. Safely hidden, he sat up and put Max carefully down. He put his index finger up to his lips to indicate that they should all remain silent. Taking a nervous breath he knelt up and looked cautiously over the top of the barrels.

Suddenly his eyes widened with astonishment. It was the crystal!

*

The alien time craft arrived over Dover castle a few minutes after James arrived. Foolishly not bothering to scan, the boy failed to realise that he had been followed by the craft! As soon as it had fully materialised, it automatically activated its stealth-mode and became transparent. In the pitch dark of the night it could not be seen.

The robot pilot operated the complex controls with cold, calculating precision; determined to locate TALON and the crystal as soon as possible. Hovering silently above the castle at a safe distance, its advanced scanners swept the area.

Soon its instruments detected the magnetic signal emitted by TALON, and the energy signature of the crystal. However its instruments struggled to cope with the strength of the Leo crystal, as it pulsated like the heartbeat of a proud king of the jungle.

Following its orders the robot steered the craft lower to observe what was happening.

Next the craft's complex recording equipment hummed into life, seeing everything that was happening.

Suddenly an alarm sounded on one of the control panels. The robot responded by focusing the recording equipment onto what had triggered the alarm.

Automatically the video-scanner zoomed in on the shape of Max and flashed another warning on the control panel.

The screen below the scanner flashed the words...
CONFIRMATION: SUBJECT IDENTIFIED AS MAXIMUS PRIME.

*

James saw that it was a tall woman who was carrying the Leo crystal. She held it in front of her with both hands. The crystal was made of Sapphire, clear blue, hexagonal in shape and the size of a large fist. It was giving off a strange glow which alternated from blue to red every few seconds. James thought that it looked a bit like the light on a police car.

"It is as I told you, Master," whispered TALON in a quiet electronic voice. "It is the next of the fire sign crystals and is the second hardest mineral known to man. I am not fully clear what its powers are, but it is supposed to provide strength and aid victory."

James nodded in silent understanding. Despite having destroyed the Dark Zodiac and aliens, he remembered Max's warning that each crystal had a guardian with powers to protect it. He also recalled that not all the previous guardians, whom he had met, had been willing to give up the crystals!

"So this is midnight on 1 August 1588? King Philip II of Spain is trying to invade England with the Spanish Armada but will fail. England is led by Queen Elizabeth I. So why are we at Dover castle?"

"The crystal must be here for a purpose, Master. Remember that you are getting each one in a sequence that creates historic events as we know them in your own time period," responded TALON.

"What is happening now?" interrupted Max, almost ready to complete its power-up.

James sneaked another look up over the barrels again. This time he saw two other women were following the one carrying the crystal. They were dressed like her, in long flowing white robes. They also reminded James of the clothes worn by Davius and his fellow High Priests in ancient Stonehenge, when he had gone in search of the Aquarius crystal.

As he watched, the three women stopped in the middle of the widest part of the castle's isolated battlement. Then the one with the crystal held it up above her head; its alternating light cast weird shadows across her face.

Now James could see her more clearly. She was in her late twenties and had long flowing red hair which cascaded over her shoulders and down to her waist. *Just like a lion's mane!*

The other two women were older; one with short blonde hair and the other with short black hair.

Suddenly the woman with red hair spoke out loud.

"I, Leo-Battle; focus the power of my crystal to protect our nation and people. I Leo-Battle, in the service of our gracious Queen Elizabeth focus the power of the crystal to cause the elements to scatter and destroy the Spanish armada!"

"Or course!" exclaimed James to TALON and Max. "The Spanish armada sailed up the English Channel ready to invade but they were shadowed by the English fleet. Suddenly bad weather and treacherous currents forced the armada to anchor off the French port of Calais. On the night of the 7th August the English floated in some burning fire ships, which scattered the Spanish fleet. The next day the Armada was pounded by English gunners off Gravelines. Then suddenly an even stronger wind blowing from the south west swept the battered armada into the North Sea. Here they were then battered by severe storms. Finally the winds forced the Spanish to abandon their invasion and they had to flee by sailing north around Scotland and then south around Ireland. Again another strong gale drove even more ships onto Irish rocks where survivors were killed by English soldiers and settlers. Of the 25,000 Spaniards who set out, less than 10,000 got home safely. Fewer than half the ships of the great armada got back to Spain.

"Queen Elizabeth and the people were jubilant. England was transformed into a world power by this victory. A thanksgiving service was held in St Paul's Cathedral in London for the delivery of the nation, and a medal was struck, with the words *'God blew and they were scattered'* inscribed on it!"

TALON hummed with excitement. "That's it, Master, Leo-Battle is about to use the power of the crystal to summon the storms. The Queen must have ordered it, and recognises the crystals power by calling it *God's wind.*"

By now Max was fully re-charged and was floating up level with the boy's head.

"In which case, once she has used the crystal to create the storms, this historic event will be successfully set on course. You will be able to take the crystal without causing problems to the time line."

At last a straight forward mission, thought James!

Suddenly a series of rifle shots rang out and the three women fell to the ground injured! The crystal dropped from

Leo-Battle's hands and rolled away, its inner glow fading rapidly!

Chapter 12

Mary did not have to sneak into her brother's bedroom, as her parents had gone out.

Instead she flung open the door and stomped into the room. What she always found annoying was that his room was bigger than hers. She always believed that their parents had allocated him the larger room in reward for him being a swat. Rather than using the extra space for fun things or cramming it with her "undesirable" friends (as she would have done if she had the space), he had half the room set up as some sort of crackpot laboratory.

She began by opening up his cupboards and drawers, systematically searching through his clothes and school work.

Then she searched under his bed, to see if anything was hidden. Still she found nothing of interest. Not even a hidden cigarette. She sighed; her brother was such a goody-goody!

Finally she went over to the tables set against the far wall; which served as his laboratory. She cursed under her breath; it looked as if most of his jumble of equipment had been removed. However, under one of the tables she could see a large cardboard box. Cautiously she stooped down, took hold of the box and cautiously slid it out.

The flaps on the top of the box were folded down tightly and taped into place. Across this James had stuck a label in red saying DO NOT OPEN! The box felt quite heavy and was giving off an odd smell. More curious than ever, she sat down cross-legged in front of the box and ripped open the top!

*

In the cellar beneath the house Davius paced up and down, a look of worry creased across his face.

He was still very concerned about James. While he thought that the boy displayed extraordinary courage and ability, he feared that his rage could break out again at any moment. Ever since the boy had become exposed to the crystals, his darker side had become stronger. Previously Davius had been able to calm him down, such as the time James unleashed the powers of the Aquarius, Libra and Gemini crystals against some school bullies in a burning barn. However the last time, when James had also used the power of the Aries crystal, the High Priest had been unable to stop him storming into the Dark Zodiac's secret underground Headquarters and destroying it.

That was why Davius had agreed with Max's idea of creating the Horoscope Matrix to shield the crystals; not just from the aliens but James as well. The High Priest was beginning to fear that James would not be able to cope when all the crystals were brought back together again. Was that the reason his ancestor in Atlantis had scattered them in the first place?

But, deep inside, Davius felt that he could trust James. The High Priest sensed that the boy's destiny was to be in the right place at the right time. That was why when the boy had saved his life during the hunt for the Aries crystal, he had trusted James with a secret mission (which even Max knew nothing about).

Neither he nor James should ever reveal to anyone anything about the four sheaths which the boy had fought so hard to get in order to save the old man. Besides, who would believe them; what James had to do to get them was even more far-fetched than anything he had done in his battles against the Dark Zodiac.

Once he had succeeded in getting the sheaths from Silbury hill, Callanish, Bryn-celli-Ddu and New Grange he had united them with their daggers kept at Stonehenge. The combined power had saved Davius. Then they had been hidden at

Stonehenge. And he warned James that they would be vital to winning a future battle!

Now Davius realized that this was the "FINAL BATTLE" his mystery ancestor had mentioned when they were spying on them in Atlantis! Even if James succeeded in battling to get all twelve crystals, the four daggers Davius had ordered hidden at Stonehenge would be needed to win a thirteenth battle!

The quest was taking yet another unexpected and deadly twist!

*

"Someone's shot Leo-Battle!" exclaimed James from behind the wooden barrels.

All three women were lying on the ground motionless in the flickering light of distant flaming torches. The crystal had stopped rolling away from Leo-Battle's limp hands and come to a stop in the middle of the battlement; its inner glow fading fast.

James jumped up and ran across to where the women lay. "They are all dead, Master," cautioned TALON solemnly, scanning from its position on his belt.

Crouching over Leo-Battle, James looked down at the lifeless body and then looked around in all directions. "Who fired those shots? They must want to stop her from summoning the storms to smash the Spanish fleet!"

"Stop talking and get the crystal!" ordered Max, flying into view. "You must get it now!"

"NO! It's mine!" shouted Leo-Battle as she suddenly sat up, her eyes wide open. Astonished, James fell over onto his back and scrambled away.

"You're dead!"

"I was dead for a moment, boy. But remember that I am Leo-Battle. I have the constitution of a lion and just like a cat I have nine lives!"

Suddenly another volley of shots rang out and ricocheted all around them. James threw himself flat; the worst of the impacts bouncing off the tough molecule flexible metal of his suit. Max flew above the line of shots out of harm's way. However Leo-Battle was hit several times and slumped back to the ground again lifeless once more. Scarlet stains spreading across her white robes.

"Who's firing at us?" sounded TALON in a high-pitched electronic voice.

Scanning in all directions Max located a small group of well armed men running across the ramparts towards them. "Spaniards!" it warned. "They are obviously here to stop this woman from using the crystal to defend England from the Armada!"

Suddenly the woman sat up again; even more angry than before. "That hurt!"

"Stop moaning, you've got another seven lives left!" snapped TALON, unimpressed.

"No I haven't!" she responded, springing up into a crouching position and pushing back her mass of red hair. "As my name suggests, this is not the first battle I have been in. All my spare lives have been used up. If I get killed again I'm dead and gone forever!"

Thoughtfully she put her hand onto her chest, where the blood was drying. She knew that if she was shot again, the next lot of blood would not stop!

Putting himself in front of the woman in order to protect her, James pointed at the crystal, "You've got to complete your mission. You must activate the crystal and create those storms!"

Suddenly the armed men emerged from the shadows; running at full speed towards them.

"Do something, Max!" shouted James; but the green ball was already whooshing towards them. It immediately started to fire bursts of energy from its single red eye.

The astonished Spaniards gasped and scattered to each side of Max in terror, as it swooped between them.

"I must get the crystal!" shouted the woman through gritted teeth and she sprang to her feet and ran towards it.

"Wait for me!" shouted James, "TALON and I can protect you!"

Before he could move, the woman using her lion-like speed and reflexes had sprinted across the battlements and reached the crystal. Triumphantly she snatched it in her right hand and stood up erect. "Now to summon the power of the storms!"

Rushing over to help her, James activated his suit's camouflage and temperature controls ready just in case they were needed.

Taking a deep breath Leo-Battle raised the crystal above her head and clasped it tightly with both hands. Once again it began to glow and throb with light and energy, sending a narrow beam vertically into the black night sky.

Across the battlements a Spanish sniper took up position, ready to fire. James saw him and leapt in front of the woman, hoping his suit would be strong enough to deflect the shot! Sensing what he was doing, she swung around and stepped to one side; putting herself in the line of fire to protect the boy. Suddenly a shot rang out.

James stood up in front of her, just as the projectile struck her in the back. She jerked unexpectedly and began to totter towards him. He saw the new red stain spreading across her chest. He looked up at her face and saw the life draining out of her eyes for the last time. She gave a whispered gasp, "promise me you will use the crystal to protect us from the Armada..."

Then she collapsed into his arms.

He took her full weight and lowered her to the ground, the crystal clattering to the floor again.

More shots rang out and ricocheted on the floor around him.

Chapter 13

Mary opened the box like a mad thing; ripping aside the flaps and the label in red saying DO NOT OPEN!

The moment the pressure of the lid was released, the top burst open and a fountain of green goo exploded all over her.

The foul smelling mixture covered her head and shoulders; sliding slowly down her face in green and yellow rivulets. Sitting cross-legged in front of the box, she had taken the full impact of James's burglar-deterrent, and not a drop had landed in the bedroom!

Attached to the spring mechanism which had unleashed the goo, was a label printed TOLD YOU NOT TO OPEN ME!

She sat stunned into silence (something very rare for her), then angrily used both her hands to scoop the muck from her eyes. Her mind was full of ideas. Use the goo to mess up his room in revenge? Use it to mess up the house? She sighed loudly, knowing that she would get the blame anyway. Instead she folded the flaps back into position as best she could and slid the box back under the table.

Sighing even louder, she stood up and left the room in silence. By the time she got to the bathroom the awful stinking mixture had slid down the front of her favourite T-shirt and was dripping onto her legs.

She now knew more than ever that her brother was up to something; but she didn't know what.

*

Max whooshed across the battlements at head height, shooting at the Spaniards.

The one who had fired the fatal shot at Leo-Battle fell back stunned by the force of the green sphere's blast.

Taking control of the situation, Max barked orders.

"Quick, boy, use the crystal before the Spanish troops can re-group. I am still not fully re-charged and I can't hold them off forever!"

Immediately James operated the suit's camouflage mode and it turned to a stone colour to match the floor of the castle. As soon as it had completed its colour change, James reached out and picked up the crystal. It felt different from the others; heavier, sharper, and pulsating.

Standing up he held it above his head. "I am a crystal user. I call upon the power of the crystal to control the elements and summon the storms!"

Trying to hide him better, his suit suddenly changed to black and grey to blend into the shadows. To onlookers it appeared as if the crystal was floating in the air by itself!

Again Max fired a burst of energy at the darkly clad Spaniards, causing sparks to bounce off their black painted armour.

James stood virtually invisible in the darkness. He could feel the energy beginning to spread through his body like a hot tingling sensation. The crystal seemed to grow lighter as if he was becoming more powerful. He felt as if he was being swept along in a tide of hot swirling energy. No! He *must* concentrate. He must focus on the mission. He must take control of the winds. He forced himself to remember his history lessons. He must set in motion several great storms. First he must drive the Spanish fleet into Calais, and then he must scatter and blow them into the North Sea. Finally he must force them onto the Irish rocks. In his head he could see a picture of the events; as if watching the scenes in fast motion from the air. He closed his eyes, gritted his teeth and concentrated. Then he could see them! The first winds blowing the ships across to France, then the great storm scattering them and finally driving lots of ships onto the rocks! He had done it!

The storms were coming, one at a time, on the dates required to cause the most damage to the invaders. He had successfully caused another historic event to happen!

But why stop here? he thought. *Why not use the power to cause more storms! Why not engulf the world in storms; to stop all fighting? Why not use the power for his own purposes!*

He could feel himself bursting with the power of the crystal. He felt driven to keep using its power over and over again! No one could stop him...

Suddenly an ear-splitting screech filled his head and caused him to slump to the floor.

"TALON! What are you doing?" he screamed.

"Using my sonic power to bring you to your senses, Master. You were about to lose all control to the crystal!"

James felt the pain in his ears driving the energy from his body, allowing him to regain control.

Were Davius and Maximus-Prime right? He was a *crystal user*, rather than just a *collector*! He had almost succumbed to the evil side of their power several times before. Once in the barn fire and recently in his revenge attack on the Dark Zodiac HQ.

He wished that Davius, the High Priest from Stonehenge was with him. Of all the people that he had met so far on this quest, James felt that he was the one who could best advise and guide him.

*

Close by, but completely undetected, the time craft hovered motionless like a bird of prey. The robot on board observed and recorded everything with uncanny accuracy.

It had identified the boy's mysterious helper, Maximus-Prime, and witnessed the boy almost falling under the evil side of the crystal's power.

Moving the craft closer, it locked its tracking equipment onto the TALON and waited; its single electronic eye blinking slowly.

As it had suspected, it was not long before the boy, his TALON, Maximus-Prime and the Leo crystal vanished as they *time burst* back to their own period.

Operating the craft's controls, the robot and the time craft also vanished in a blast of intense light, leaving no trace behind. In the coming days the storms would rage and the Armada would fail. History would follow its designed course.

Chapter 14

Davius turned around with a fright as the cellar filled with rainbow light and a rush of air. It seemed as if James and Max had only been away a matter of minutes. He still found the quirks of time travel difficult to get used to!

James stepped out of the light and landed on his feet with ease; he was growing more confident with each journey. Max however bounced out and rolled across the dusty floor. Spinning several times it came to a stop and uttered an electronic groan.

"I am not designed for time travel. Now I will have to do a complete systems check before I can go again. You will have to go after the Sagittarius crystal without me."

"I will go with you," reassured Davius, patting the boy on the shoulder.

"Best if you do," mumbled the boy, as he placed the Leo crystal into the Horoscope Matrix. "The dangerous effects of the crystal almost took control of me again. Who knows what I would have done if TALON had not hit me with a sonic blast and snapped me out of its influence?"

Davius cast a knowing look at Max; their secret concerns were becoming true. Someone would have to be with James at all times on the quest.

"Was it difficult to get this crystal? Did you encounter a Leo guardian?" the old man questioned.

TALON responded on behalf of James, sensing its master's weariness. "*Yes* there was a fight. *Yes* it was dangerous. *Yes* we managed to get the crystal. *Yes* we ensured a key historic event took place. *Yes* we encountered Leo-Battle. *No* she did not survive the fight; and *no* we did not kill her!"

Davius rolled his eyes. "OK! OK! *I get the picture* as you would say!"

The High Priest felt that he could cut the atmosphere in the cellar with a knife. He was anxious to make sure that everyone was well, especially James in his present state of mind!

*

The time craft battled its way through the vortex of time travel after James on his return journey; however it was much more difficult than the robot had expected.

Whatever device the boy used was very sophisticated; and was impossible to follow in real-time. The best the robot and the tracking equipment could do was record the energy signatures left behind the boy and the TALON and hope to replicate them at a later date! It was confident that if pursuit was impossible, then interception might be possible instead. Deciding to terminate its pursuit of the boy and TALON, it activated the homing device inserted into its body and sent the saucer-shaped craft back to the aliens' headquarters!

*

James sat in the cellar, taking stock. Getting the Leo crystal had proved much easier than he had expected. However he was still stunned by the sacrifice which Leo-Battle had made for him. It was as if the good guardians of the crystals seemed to sense that his mission had the greatest importance and were determined to protect him. Davius was a clear example, as was the Gemini twins from ancient Egypt and the Libra guardian from the Tower of London.

He sighed out loud; at least each mission should be less complicated than before; now that he had destroyed the Aliens and the Dark Zodiac in their secret underground base, they would not be chasing him any more!

From now on he would only have to deal with any crystal guardians who might want to keep hold of their crystal!

At least James felt good about destroying the Dark Zodiac base. They had taken over a former secret government underground city known as the *"Burlington bunker"*. It was a 35 acre cold war city 40 metres beneath the town of Corsham. Built in the late 1950s the massive complex was designed to hold up to 4,000 government staff in the event of a Russian nuclear attack. It was to be the emergency war HQ and was blast proof and self-sufficient. It had its own hospital, canteens, accommodation, stores, lake and largest telecommunication centre in Britain. It was closed down at the end of the cold war in 1991.

A separate part of it was also rumoured to be UK's version of the USA's top secret area 51. The local RAF Rudloe Manor site at Corsham was the Government's main headquarters for recording all UFO activity in its Flying Complaints Flight; before the RAF base was shut down by the Government in the late 1990s.

When James exploded into the base, the mysterious leader of the Dark Zodiac was revealed as ATOSS; the result of a secret cold war experiment to create a super-soldier which went wrong.

James discovered that Secret deals had been made between key figures in the Government and the aliens.

This secret site hidden within a secret Government cold war bunker became the place where aliens and humans met and plotted.

Advanced technology was given to the group by the aliens and a secret society was created to take over the world.

ATOSS revealed that the aliens knew of ancient Atlantis and had physical evidence of its existence, of which humans knew nothing. They had discovered an ancient stone tablet and the existence of the twelve crystals and their awesome power.

When James had confronted ATOSS, he discovered the super soldier had the ancient tablet. ATOSS flaunted it at

James and then destroyed it in front him. James realised that he had seen the tablet before. Back in 2250 BC Egypt, searching for the Gemini crystal; before it had been hidden, to await discovery by British explorers in the nineteenth century! Now he realised where it had come from and how an ancestor of Davius would create it. He cursed that ATOSS was the one to shatter ten thousand years of history!

While in the secret underground base James had also discovered that the aliens had provided them with a time craft to go and get each crystal. All they needed was the ancient coin with the coded crystal locations engraved on.

But James had got it first and with Max and TALON's help had begun to get the crystals before they could!

So they decided to attack James at home! The thought of it caused him to clench his fists so tightly that his knuckles went white. That was what had sent him into an uncontrollable rage. That was what had driven him to take the four crystals he had and use them against the enemy. But the crystals had taken control of him.

ATOSS may have shattered the tablet but James then defeated ATOSS! However at the height of his crystal-fuelled rage, an alien had attacked James, accidentally snapping him out of his rage.

Sitting in silence in the cellar, James shuddered as he recalled the first time he had looked upon an alien. A hideous creature with long, writhing tentacles resembling a giant man-sized jelly fish, but was surrounded by a solid transparent bubble, like a huge goldfish bowl. He soon discovered that the creatures communicated by telepathy.

James recalled how the alien had boasted that it was a member of the race planning to take over the earth. They were a dying race and there were only a few of them left. He shuddered again as he remembered it bragging that they needed humans for food and to re-build their slave-armies.

The aliens' own planet died long ago. For centuries they had been searching for a suitable world to colonise. It had confessed that they only had one star craft left, and needed to make secret alliances with corrupt members of earth governments. James smiled to himself; the aliens may have discovered the *history* of Atlantis, but he had *been there and seen it* for himself!

In his confrontation with the alien leader he had also uncovered why the aliens couldn't go after the crystals themselves. *Their bodies cannot withstand the physical pressures of time travel!* He chuckled to himself. That is why they designed the time craft for the Dark Zodiac to use on their behalf.

In the final battle James had not only triumphed and killed them all, but he was proud that he had not revealed anything about Maximus-Prime, how he had been given TALON and told where the coin was. Nor how he created his own time travel device or the secret of the mysterious black gas he had discovered and his everlasting light bulb experiment.

He sat back and smiled to himself; things had been grim. But if he kept his cool and resisted the temptation of misusing the crystals he should finish the quest in no time at all.

"Are you ready to go after the next crystal, Master?" interrupted TALON.

Chapter 15

The time craft reappeared in the alien's base with a flash of light and blast of air.

The robot pilot opened the door in the side of the saucer and stepped out. Its shiny skeleton and mass of cables reflected the green light of the chamber's walls. The single unblinking red eye in its metal skull scanned the chamber around it.

As soon as it was clear of the craft the auto-operation device in the tiny homing beacon in the robot's chest plate sent the craft back to its alternative reality until it was needed again.

Suddenly a door opened in the side of the chamber and several of the alien travel spheres floated in.

"Did you get a crystal, or find out where the boy's secret hideout is?" probed the leader using telepathy.

"No, my Masters. But I have other information which is of equal importance and will give you victory!"

The constantly undulating creatures began to throb and pulsate in unison; their travel spheres floating around the room excitedly. Their jelly-like bodies began to glow with different colours; the faint light coming from deep inside each creature growing stronger.

*

Mary was showered, dry and changed within ten minutes. (Something highly unusual; as her father constantly moaned at her for taking an hour in the bathroom!) She had replaced her ruined best T-shirt with her next best top and next favourite skirt. Leaning against the bathroom wall she bent down; her boots were alright and she stomped her feet down into them hard and laced them up.

No matter how hard she tried she could not shake the strange images of James from her mind. It was as if someone had blotted out a section of her memory.

However without anything to trigger her memories she could not push on with her investigation.

Suddenly she thought of the garden shed! It had been abandoned for years, yet she was sure that she had seen her brother hanging around there during the last few weeks.

Five metres below her in the cellar, Max, James, TALON and Davius were completely unaware of what was happening in the house above. Having used the shed as his first temporary HQ, James had abandoned it when the aliens had almost discovered him there. He had cleared all his equipment out of the tiny wooden building and with Max's help moved it into the bricked-up cellar.

Little did Mary know that it had only been the quick thinking of Max that had saved her life from a hunter-killer robot. On an earlier mission an alien robot had detected TALON in the shed, but had prepared to attack her instead!

Completely unaware of all this and with nothing else to do, Mary bounded down the stairs to the kitchen. She would grab a snack and then go and investigate the shed.

*

"Are you ready to go, Master James?" snapped the know-it-all voice of TALON.

"Master is to get the Sagittarius Crystal next. It is the last of the three fire sign crystals and is made of Turquoise. It should be rounded in shape and egg sized. I am not fully clear what the Sagittarius crystal's powers are, but it is supposed to enhance intuition and psychic skills. My sensors should easily locate it. It should be a light blue with green streaks through it and be rounded."

James wondered to himself exactly what power its guardian had to protect it.

66

"Where and when are we going to get this crystal TALON?"

"Master, the sequence instructs that we will have to go back 64 million, 854 thousand years. This period marks the end of the Cretaceous period. The location is what is now called the Yucatan Peninsula in Mexico."

Max was partly re-charged but far from ready to operate at peak performance yet.

"Do you want me to use one of the crystals to speed up your healing process?" offered the boy.

"That will not be necessary!" it snapped back, not wishing the boy to have any more contact with the crystals than he had already got. Instead it floated over to the Horoscope Matrix and touched its glowing energy field. "Being next to the matrix will enable me to siphon off some of the crystals' healing powers."

Davius stepped forward and put his hand on James's shoulders. "You look fatigued, boy. Go and touch the matrix energy field yourself; to benefit from its healing powers."

James nodded and walked across the cellar and put a hand into the energy field. Although he was not touching the crystals directly, he could feel their power. After a few minutes he pulled his hand out.

"That felt good. I'm ready to get the next crystal now!"

*

The alien base hummed with activity and anticipation. In the main control chamber seven aliens hovered in their individual travel spheres waiting to get a full report back from the robot. The robot stood on a raised dais in the centre of the chamber; while above it hovered the alien leader.

"Proceed with the report!" it commanded by telepathy.

Without a word a three-dimensional holographic image appeared in the air above the robot.

Firstly a life size image of Max appeared. On seeing its image all the aliens gasped mentally in union.

"Maximus-Prime!" exclaimed the leader out loud. "So that is where it got to. And if it is helping the boy, it explains where the boy has been getting all that technical help from. It explains where the boy got the TALON from and how he knew where to get the coin with the crystal locations from."

The other aliens glowed and pulsated with anger. "The mystery is solved!" they chanted in union.

The leader floated higher into the chamber. "But I wonder if the boy knows Maximus-Prime's true motives?"

The image of Max suddenly vanished and was replaced by views of James holding the Leo crystal, as he lost control to its power.

"So the boy is still not able to use their power without losing control!" thought the leader out loud. "If we can capture him I am certain that he can be tricked into helping us!"

Next there appeared a stream of data, which swirled and twisted like the coloured whirlpool of light.

"At last a visual record of the type of time vortex which the boy's time suit uses! With this information we will be able to follow the TALON better."

The leader stopped transmitting its thoughts for a moment and rotated around the swirling images. Its throbbing body glowed again and its tentacles wriggled around inside the transparent travel sphere like a mass or worms. "If this detailed download is correct it may be possible to *intercept* the boy as he makes his next time burst."

One of the other aliens floated up level with the leader, as if to challenge it.

"Even if we can do as you suggest our new Dark Zodiac super humans will not be fully grown by then. Even if we use accelerated growth compounds on them and their genetically enhanced bodies can withstand the strain; they are clones and will only mature with the powers they have inherited!"

The leader span around to face its questioner. "I agree. That is why it is essential for us to turn the boy's mind against his friends, and trick him into helping us get the crystals! With this detailed download entered into our instruments we should be able to intercept the boy as he makes his next time burst and *bring him here!"*

Chapter 16

"I still don't understand why I can't get several crystals in one go?" probed James as he got ready for his next time jump.

Max pondered for a moment; much as it would make sense to get them all by travelling directly from one time period to the next before returning to the cellar, it was concerned that James would fall under their influence again.

"No, you should still get them one at a time for now. Once you get the last of the fire signs; we could re-consider."

James did not reply directly; but walked over to one of the work benches. "I have also been thinking about a way to boost my suit's time travel power. I was thinking about using my remaining everlasting light bulb to open a time door and then use my suit's power to time burst through the hole. That should increase the speed of my jump. The black gas in the bulb combined with the quantity of gas my body and suit absorbed should magnify the power."

Keen to put his idea into practice, it only took him a few minutes to set up the bulb and its holder. Throwing the switch, he stood back as a swirling black hole opened in mid air. He could not control where the time door went to; but be *could* control where his suit went to. If he jumped through with a specific location programmed into his suit, he should get to where he wanted twice as fast.

*

Mary had found her way through the back of the house into the yard and was striding out towards the bottom end of the garden. She knew that her father had an old shed somewhere beyond the overgrown plants and hedges. She recalled that she had seen her brother sneaking in this direction several times over the last few weeks and wanted to get to the bottom of things.

The shed was partly concealed behind a mass of brambles and plants which had gone wild. Picking up a stick which was lying on the ground she bashed aside some of the thickest brambles until she could reach the door. To her surprise she found that a lot of the brambles had been discreetly fastened across the door to make it look as if the shed had not been opened for years! Suspecting her mad-scientist brother's handiwork was hiding something important in the shed, she grasped the door knob and pulled hard. The door swung open far easier than she expected, and she stumbled backwards falling into her father's age-old compost heap.

Cursing at the top of her voice she staggered back to her feet and looked down at her bottom. Now her second favourite skirt was stained with green and black slime!

Cursing under her breath she blamed her brother. No matter how hard she tried, she could not shake the strange images of James from her mind.

She slammed aside the wooden door and stepped inside, just in time to trigger her brother's other security device. The plastic bucket of stale water fell over head and drenched her completely!

Unable to see because of the bucket over her head, she stumbled forward into the empty shed and fell flat on her face. The bucket muffled her curses, until she sat up and pulled it off. Muttering, but now beyond rage, she looked down at her drenched body. Her second best top was now ruined!

Suddenly she noticed the outline of a trap door in the wooden floor of the shed. Leaning forward she ran her fingers around its edge until she could get a good grip; then lifted it up. Smiling with satisfaction she at last knew that she was on to something and peered down into the hole. To her surprise she found that the door concealed a hidden compartment between the floor boards and the soil beneath. Several areas had been cut into the ground, and she could see marks where boxes had been stored.

To her dismay there was nothing in the compartment. James must have removed everything! But where to?

Suddenly she stopped and put her hand down into the secret compartment again. She could feel a strange tingling sensation. It was faint, but she could definitely feel a slight electrical current; as if whatever James had previously hidden there had left behind some of its energy.

*

Having thrown the switch, James stood back as a swirling black hole opened in mid air in the cellar and grew in size. He remembered what he had seen in Atlantis; somehow they had made certain he would find the mysterious black gas which provided the power to time travel.

He knew he could not control where the time door went to; but he *could* control where his suit went to. If he jumped through with a specific location programmed into his suit, he should get to where he wanted twice as fast.

Max hovered alongside him. "Are you sure about this? Doubling your power in this disjointed way could act like a beacon to others who can detect time travellers. To those with the right equipment, it would be like advertising yourself as you time burst!

"Not only that, but the wider range of the zone, more objects could be accidentally sucked into the time vortex. Others who are close by could be sucked into the vortex!"

Suddenly there was a roar like that of a monstrous beast from the swirling black hole. Before anyone could react; James, Max, Davius and TALON were sucked into it. Their screaming voices could be heard echoing; until they faded to nothing.

Moments later the safety self-timer on the light bulb rang out and the bulb switched off. Instantly the time door shrank and faded to nothing.

BUT THE FIVE CRYSTALS REMAINED SAFE IN CELLAR, CONTAINED IN THE HOROSCOPE MATRIX!

*

In the garden shed Mary still had her hands in the secret compartment. Unknown to her, James had previously stored the light bulb, TALON and several crystals there, before moving them to the cellar. Unknown to James, there was still a faint electromagnetic residue in the compartment.

Unfortunately for Mary, the residue was close enough to the cellar and her brother's enhanced black hole. Close enough to be connected to its increased range and suck her into its swirling time vortex. With a startled gasp she vanished from the dusty shed in a flash of rainbow light!

Chapter 17

James, TALON, Max and Davius were thrown out of the swirling time door in unison and emerged in a large circular cell. The room's walls were metallic and glittered as if sprinkled with gold. The front portion of the cell was transparent and through it they could make out large shifting shadows.

"Where are we?" spluttered James.

Max was wobbling, its internal chemical circuits struggling to recover from the unplanned journey.

"I think we were sucked into the time door you opened, James," suggested Davius. "It is as if someone snatched us just before you could make your next time burst!"

James looked all around, trying to find a door in the glittering walls.

"Where and when are we, TALON?"

The little ball whirred for a few seconds, "We were definitely intercepted and drawn here, Master. However my instruments also tell me that we have *not* travelled through time. We appear to have been pulled to a different location on present day earth."

"In which case I can get us out of here just as quick!" replied the boy, operating his wrist control. Nothing happened.

"I don't understand? Why can't I simply location jump us out of here?"

TALON whirred and responded. "Firstly the door opened by your light bulb has automatically closed behind us; preventing anyone from using it to get into the cellar. Secondly at least the five crystals are safe in the cellar, and were not sucked here with us! However we cannot use your light bulb to get back to the cellar either!"

"I don't need the light bulb to location jump!" snapped James as he tried using the wrist controls again, but nothing happened.

"Sorry, Master, but the powerful equipment which sucked us here, is also powerful enough to keep us here. My instruments tell me that this cell is surrounded by a force field, which stops you from either time bursting or location jumping."

"Trapped like rats!" cursed Davius; his face fixed into a worried scowl.

*

The alien behind the large screen in the control chamber watched James with fascination. It recognised the boy from their last confrontation in the Dark Zodiac's secret underground complex. Was it really this earth-boy who had thwarted their plans for world domination? Was this truly the person referred to on the ancient stone tablet, who was destined to get the crystals?

The alien leader's jelly-like bulk quivered with a mixture of curiosity and anticipation. It could sense that James was filled with confusion and anger. It could see TALON was strapped to his side! Now there would be no way for the boy to stop the aliens from learning the location of the crystals!

The leader turned its attention to studying the other captives in the cell. Maximus-Prime hovered uncertainly in the corner, clearly re-energising itself as fast as it could. Its blotchy green artificial skin twitched and vibrated as it neared the end of the process. In the centre of the cell, standing behind James protectively, was a mysterious old man. The alien studied him for a moment, scanning his strange appearance and wisdom-filled features.

The alien would have preferred to interrogate them one at a time to discover everything they knew. However it needed to turn the boy from good to evil as soon as possible!

Mary appeared out of mid air and tumbled into a dark corridor with a thud. She lay shivering for several minutes on the smooth metal floor, not daring to open her eyes.

Her heart pounded in her chest so loudly that it sounded like large drums playing in her head. Rivers of sweat soaked her body like second skin. Eventually her heavy breathing began to slow and the swirling sensation in her head faded.

Even with her eyes closed she knew that she was no longer in the shed. The smell was different. It was a strange mix of animal odours occasionally overwhelmed by a hospital smell. The floor under her outstretched body was hard and metallic; definitely not the shed.

The sounds were also wrong. All she could make out were the constant echo of humming equipment in the distance. Definitely not her parents' garden. How she wished that she had not bothered to investigate her brother!

Taking a deep breath she opened her eyes.

A shocked gasp stifled her scream. She was in a long dark metal corridor, lit only by an occasional green glow. The corridor was only big enough to crawl through; it must be some kind of air purifying pipe.

Tears welled in her eyes; where was she and how did she get here!

*

James was about to start testing how sturdy the cell walls were by kicking them, when the transparent screen on the far wall slid aside with a low hiss. As the opening was revealed he saw that it was filled by a row of creatures hovering in transparent spheres.

"The aliens!" gasped James, his wide eyes filled with alarm, as he recognised the creatures floating in their transparent travel spheres.

"But I thought that you had killed them all in the Dark Zodiac's underground base?" spluttered Davius.

"Can't trust you to do anything right!" snapped TALON half joking nervously.

Max, still recovering, floated across to James and hovered alongside him. Davius moved around to the other side; they would stand together and fight. Discreetly Max circuit tested its defensive weapons. In another minute it would be able to blast the aliens out of their flying transport spheres!

The leading alien floated a little closer towards them and then turned to Max. "Your weapons will not work in the cell. In fact none of you can defend yourselves now you are trapped in our base!"

"I destroyed you!" shouted back James in defiance. "I fought you all and destroyed you all!"

The alien floated closer and focused its thoughts at the boy. "Not so. The base you destroyed belonged to the Dark Zodiac and its leader ATOSS. We helped them build it, but we were not living there. We have our own base here; where you are now trapped. I teleported out of the Dark Zodiac base a milisecond before it exploded."

James wobbled with despair and leaned against Davius for support. "Then all the aliens still survive and have still got their star craft!"

The alien glowed brightly and changed to a different colour. "Indeed and you are in that craft right now. We concealed it at a secret underground location on earth and are using it as our base. We have built a whole series of tunnels and chambers around it. This is a place you call Easter Island. And despite our setbacks we still intend to take over this planet. We need lots of people for food and as slaves."

"How?" sneered Davius, cursing under his breath that he was not able to draw upon the power of Stonehenge and blast his way out of here. If he had still been in the British Isles he could draw upon the power of the Ley lines and tap into the energy which connected ancient stone circles. However, trapped on an alien space craft hidden under an island in the Pacific Ocean, he was not able to tap into any power source!

The leader continued; revelling in its complete control of the situation. "We had already decided that ATOSS and his team were not up to the job of getting the crystals; even before James destroyed them and their base. We are now re-creating the twelve super humans here on this ship. There are always selfish humans willing to volunteer to be genetically engineered and cloned; for the promise of power. With them as our warrior-slaves we will be able to get all the crystals this time."

James recalled what he had seen in the other base before he had destroyed it.

Twelve transparent cubicles; one for each of the super villains, one representing each sign of the zodiac! He recalled seeing a different astrology symbol on each cubical. And inside most of them he saw the shadow of a figure.

The alien leader hovered a bit further into the cell. "We are able to take normal humans and genetically engineer them into super humans. Then we take a micro-biological-sample which allows us to create clone-type replacements whenever the original is destroyed."

James recalled looking inside one of the cubicles and seeing a figure that was a grotesque mutation wrapped in wet bandages with pipes and wires extending from it.

"How are you going to get the crystals?" demanded Davius stepping forward defiantly. Despite having never seen anything like the aliens before, he recalled James's description.

"We will use the TALON of course," it responded, changing colour and flexing its slimy wet tentacles.

"Think again, you ugly slimy heap of..." snapped back the little ball clipped to James's belt. But the sphere found that as it tried to fly free of its clip, it was unable to move. The force field encircling the cell was suppressing its movement abilities as well!

"Be patient, my little tracker; soon you and your master will *willingly* get all the crystals for us," responded the alien. Almost gloating, the hovering creature rotated its travel sphere and faced Max. Its quivering jelly fish-like body stroked itself with its mass of wet tentacles and directed all its thoughts at Max.

"You may have fooled the boy and old man; but I think that it's time your new-found friends all learned the truth about you; isn't it Maximus-Prime!"

Slowly the alien rotated to face Davius and James. "You see, we already know Maximus-Prime. And we also know that he has been lying to you!"

Chapter 18

Mary suppressed another scream and closed her eyes. Wherever she was she would not get out by lying in the dark and snivelling. She looked ahead of her and then behind her. In both directions all she could see was a long dark metal corridor, lit only by an occasional green glow. It reminded her of the sort of air-purifying pipe that criss-crossed the hospital where her mother worked. She decided to move forward, as there were more patches of green light that way. The pipe was only big enough to crawl through; but luckily she was slim enough to do it.

Tears welled in her eyes; where was she and how did she get here?

Sniffing deeply she gathered her senses and crawled forward into the darkness, hoping to reach a patch of light, or better still a way out!

After what seemed ages she finally reached one of the patches of green light. On the left of the pipe there was a metal grill covering a hole too small for her to get through. Looking through, Mary could see a room that looked like a laboratory. To one side of the room she could see the shadows of people moving. She was about to shout for help when one of the shapes came into view.

With a gasp of horror she stifled her scream by clamping her hands over her mouth. Walking into the room were several human shaped robots!

Her eyes bulging with horror, she stared at the metallic figures as they silently strode up to several control consoles and began to operate them. Desperate not to cry out in fear, she pressed her chin upwards with one hand and continued to clamp the other over her mouth.

Taking deep breaths she gradually brought her panic under control. Now her main concern was to remain hidden until she could find a way out of the pipe. Turning away from the grilled opening, she continued to crawl down the pipe into the darkness.

*

The Alien hovered closer to Max and wriggled within its travel sphere; as if taking great pleasure from stunning the prisoners with its words. Then it rotated and faced James and Davius.

"We already know Maximus-Prime and we know that he has been lying to you!"

James shook his head in defiance. "How could you? He is from a hundred years in the future!"

The alien leader pulsated and flexed its tentacles, as if controlling its silent laughter.

"Not so. You see my race is called the Zentoria; and as you know we are the last of our race. The few of us that remain have been travelling through space on this star ship searching for a new world. We found this planet and made contact with corrupt elements within the world's Governments. We then discovered your planet's secret history and the ancient crystals…"

"I know all that!" interrupted James angrily. "Max came back from the future. A future where you have succeeded in taking over. My task is to change the course of future events and stop you!"

The alien glowed a deep red with restrained anger and then continued.

"Wrong! What you do not know is that Maximus-Prime is NOT from the future. It is from the present and is a member of a rival alien race called the Metval!

"We Zentoria were chasing a Metval star ship to finish them off after long war. It is the war which has reduced our two races to near extinction. But our space fleet was also destroyed in the battle; only our craft remained. Maximus-Prime was the sole survivor from the Metval craft. In fact it is the sole survivor of the Metvals. For a long time after the war we wandered through space. Eventually discovered the earth and landed here.

"However, Maximus-Prime had been following us in secret. It also landed on earth and hid. Over the years it has secretly been monitoring our activities and our agreements with the human conspirators. Eventually it learned of our plans to get the crystals and rebuild our race. However it is in direct conflict with us. Whatever it told you to get your help, was a complete pack of lies!"

James narrowed his eyes and slowly turned to look at Max. The green sphere simply hovered in silence; not making any attempt to deny the alien's accusations.

"Is this true, Max?"

Max remained silent for a moment and then narrowed its big red eye. "It is all true…"

Davius gasped and James stumbled backwards; to be propped up by the old man.

"So the threat of a future alien victory was a lie to trick me into helping you?" the boy finally responded. "All that stuff about my family being among the first to be rounded up and eaten by the aliens was made up!"

"Yes."

"Why?"

"You see, boy, I was able to decipher a lot of the stone tablet. I believe it is your destiny to get the crystals and I needed your help to get them. But I saw how humans betray their own kind, so I decided to make up the threat to your family; in order to trick you into helping me."

"But why do YOU need them?" retorted Davius. "You said that once you had them all you would destroy them so no one, including the aliens, could use them for evil?"

82

"Simple. Once I had them all I would use them to destroy the last of the Zentorias. Then I was going to destroy the crystals."

James stepped forward and thrust his face close to Max's. Anger was rising inside the young boy; just like the last time, when he had lost control to the crystals.

"So it boils down to two rival alien races; one lot are living computers and the other lot are giant jelly fish, tricking humans into helping them get the crystals to fight one last battle."

"Yes," responded Max. The other alien pulsated within its travel sphere and confirmed the boy's accusation using telepathy.

James clenched his fists. "So, Max, when I brought you back from the future it was a trick as well?"

Max narrowed its eye again. "Yes it was an elaborate deception for me to get close and keep an eye on you. When you rescued me from the tunnels it was a trick. It *was* my secret sanctuary, but it was not in the future. It was in an abandoned sewer deep under present day Paris. The explosions, fighting and the metallic spider were all made by me and timed to go off once you arrived to rescue me…"

James was at breaking point, he could feel the dark anger swelling up inside, like an expanding balloon. If he lost control he might never be able to switch back to his good self again!

The alien leader floated away from Max and directed its attention at Davius.

"I also sense that this old man has been helping Maximus-Prime deceive you…"

"What!" exclaimed the boy, on the edge of uncontrollable rage.

Davius hesitated and then nodded. "I knew nothing about Max's true origin or its secret aim; but I did agree to its dual use of the Horoscope Matrix…"

"What dual use?" snapped the boy, disbelieving his ears.

"When Max built the matrix, it was to hide the energy of the crystals so no one would be able to trace it to your cellar.

However we were so worried that you were falling under the evil side of the crystals' energy, that the matrix also stopped you from using the crystals when you brought them back."

James put his head in his hands and shook with rage. He felt utterly deceived.

Davius continued, "I now realise that Max was only doing this to save the crystals' energy for itself. So once you had got them all, they would be at maximum strength.

"Yes, James; I reluctantly deceived you. But my deception was genuine; to save the world from you if you went out of control. But like you I was also deceived by Max's true intentions."

James lowered his hands from his face and scowled back. "You may have been genuine, but you still lied to me! I can't trust any of you any more!"

The anger building in him like a kettle about to boil, he looked down at TALON.

"Did you know any of this, TALON?"

"No, Master. My memory only starts from the moment Maximus-Prime activated me and sent me to help you get the coin and start the quest for the first crystal!"

"It tells the truth," interrupted the alien leader. "The TALON is a unique device invented by the Metval. Maximus-Prime adapted it to decode the coins inscriptions and show you where the crystals are hidden."

Suddenly James began to twitch and shake uncontrollably.

"The boy's having a fit…" gasped Davius moving forward to help him.

The alien swooped in between them and stopped the old man in his tracks. "Do not touch him! He belongs to us now!"

"What do you mean?" responded the High Priest.

"Your lies and deceptions have pushed his young mind over the edge."

"Over the edge?" stuttered Davius.

Finally Max spoke as if waking up from a trance. "The Zentoria leader means that the boy has finally succumbed to his darker side. We have lost him to evil…"

As if in response, James suddenly stopped shaking and stood up erect again. "This planet and its people do not deserve to be saved. I will get the crystals for myself!"

Chapter 19

James sneered at his friends. "You have all betrayed me. Why should I risk my life to save you or humanity? It is not worth it. I will get all the remaining crystals and use them for what I want!" his eyes were like dark pits of anger; no longer those of a school boy.

"No you won't!" exclaimed the alien leader out loud.

Before anyone could move, a wide energy beam descended from the ceiling and surrounded the boy! He was held motionless.

"You may have succumbed to the evil side of the crystals' influence, but I want you to work for us; not do what you want!" boomed the alien.

The creature issued several mental commands and one of the scientific-robots strode towards James. It was carrying a metal collar in one hand. It stopped behind the boy and placed the metal device around his neck, snapping it shut with a loud click.

The alien rotated closer to him and flexed its tentacles; slowly sliding them down the inside of the transparent travel sphere, in delight. "You are now under our control. If you do not get the Sagittarius crystal and bring it back to us here, the collar will detonate and kill you. While you are wearing it, it will also transmit your location to us at all times."

Suddenly the energy beam disappeared and James could move again. His new evil personality realised that he would have to do as the aliens ordered; for now!

The alien floated away; back into the main control room.

"I have assigned a hunter-killer robot to go with you on the mission. It will help you overcome the guardian of the

Sagittarius crystal; if there is one. The robot will also make certain that you carry out my orders!"

James said nothing, merely nodding in acceptance of the task.

Making sure that TALON was securely in position on his belt; he strode out of the cell and stood next to the hunter-killer robot.

"TALON, confirm once again where we have to go next," said the boy calmly, his anger now replaced by quiet cunning.

TALON repeated the information it had issued in the cellar earlier.

"Master, the sequence instructs that we will have to go back 64 million, 854 thousand years. This period marks the end of the Cretaceous period. The location is what is now called the Yucatan Peninsula in Mexico.

"Master is to get the Sagittarius Crystal. It is the last of the three fire sign crystals and is made of Turquoise. It should be rounded in shape and egg sized. I am not fully clear what the Sagittarius crystal's powers are, but it is supposed to enhance intuition and psychic skills. My sensors should easily locate it. It should be a light blue with green streaks through it."

James looked at the alien and narrowed his eyes slightly, cunning thoughts racing through his mind. "I guess I had better get going…"

With that, he placed one hand firmly on the hunter-killer robot, so it would be connected to the vortex created by his time travel suit, and with the other hand operated his wrist controls. Immediately there was a rainbow flash and James, TALON and the robot vanished.

*

Mary continued to crawl along the air pipe as quickly as she could. The further she travelled the stronger the animal smells got. She also noticed that the air being sucked through the pipe was getting warmer. She only hoped that the robots in the laboratory had not seen her!

The next patch of green light that she came to was shining into the pipe the same way as the last one. Another hole too small for her to crawl through, covered by a metal grill. Fearing that she would see more robots, Mary edged towards the light and peered through the grill. To her surprise she was not looking down onto a small room; this time she saw a large chamber. Squinting to see better, she saw that the chamber walls were brown and green. It was as if they had grown, rather than been built. She could see strange twisting tubes and random sized holes in the curving walls of the chamber. However it was what was in the centre of the chamber that set her heart pounding again.

In the centre there was an elaborate control console, surrounded by twelve translucent cubicles. Each cubicle was twice the size of a person and shaped like a cylinder with rounded ends. Each one had strange symbols on them. Some she recognised as astrology symbols.

To her surprise she could see the shadows of shapes slowly moving inside the cubicles!

Just as she was about to put her face up against the grill to get a better look, several robots came into view.

They stopped around one of the cubicles and operated some of the controls on the supporting equipment under it. There was a hiss of machinery and suddenly the cubicle opened. Straining to see for herself, Mary pressed her nose against the grill and squinted harder. In the cubicle she could see a person, wrapped in bandages like an Egyptian mummy! Out of the wet bandages she could see various plastic tubes filed with different coloured liquids which were entering or leaving the body. Unexpectedly the mummy twitched and two robots had to hold it down while the third injected it with a large syringe.

Wincing at the sight of the needle going in, Mary made a loud gasp.

Suddenly one of the robots looked up in response; and turned towards the grill.

Horror struck she rolled out of sight and scrambled away from the opening. With grim determination she wriggled along the pipe into the darkness, desperately hoping that she had not been noticed.

*

James arrived at his destination with an awkward landing. The presence of the robot next to him unbalanced his landing. He stood motionless for a moment, until the sensations of time travel faded. TALON was still safely secured in its pouch and the robot was stood next to him.

He breathed deeply and sucked in a lungful of prehistoric air. It was foul; a mixture of rotting vegetation and dinosaur dung! James had met with dinosaurs before, but that had been the Carboniferous period 290 million years ago. This time the landscape and monsters were different. This time it was not a water-clogged swamp, instead it was a sprawling landscape jumbled with forests and open grasslands.

He still felt betrayed. His anger had long subsided; however his mind was now calm and clear. Clearly dark and clearly deceitful! He had no intention of helping the aliens. But he had every intention of helping himself!

"So, TALON, this is 64 million, 854 thousand years ago. My school books said that this period marks the end of the Cretaceous period. The period when the dinosaurs became extinct!"

TALON hummed and clicked for a moment.

"Yes, Master, this is the moment the extinction event occurs. A huge asteroid or comet smashes into the earth and wipes out most of its life forms. And this is the place it strikes!"

James looked around. In all directions were open plains mixed with lush forests. James and the robot were stood on the top of an exposed hilltop and had a panoramic view. Above the treetops in the distance he squinted into the clear blue sky. He could make out a glowing ball of light. As the sun was in the opposite side of the sky he knew that this must be the asteroid, hurtling on its collision course with the earth.

"So this is what in the twenty-first century is called the Yucatan Peninsula in Mexico," he said out loud. "This is where the asteroid strikes and the gigantic explosion takes place!"

"A good reason to stop talking and find the crystal quickly. Just as you were ordered!" interrupted the robot with a metallic voice.

James said nothing, keeping his thoughts and plans to himself.

In the distance he could hear the roar of dinosaurs getting closer as the flesh-eating ones caught his scent. In the sky the approaching asteroid was getting bigger!

The collar bit tightly into his neck, its electronic hum reminding him that one false move would blow his head off!

He had to act fast to get himself out of this mess!

Chapter 20

In the distance, James could see prehistoric reptiles swooping and circling in the sky. A bit closer he could see a herd of Triceratops grazing. These dinosaurs were like a rhinoceros, the size of an elephant, with a great armoured head. Above its eyes extended two great horns and from its armoured snout extended a shorter horn.

Elsewhere in the lush forests he could hear the roar of Tyrannosaurus Rex on the hunt.

All the while the boy's mind was racing to find a way to rid himself of the robot. Suddenly TALON broke the boy's concentration.

"I have detected the Sagittarius crystal, Master. It is five kilometres north west from here."

The alien robot turned and pointed at a hill in the distance. "There it is!"

To the boy's astonishment, he could see a tall thin tower rising from the top of a wooded hill. It resembled a lighthouse and appeared to be made out of cut stone.

"What is a building doing in this time period!" he gasped. "There were no humans alive in prehistoric periods."

"You assume the builders are human…" cautioned the robot ominously. And James wondered what new twists of history he was about to encounter on this mission. He also wondered to himself, exactly what power the crystal's guardian had to protect it!

The robot began to stride down the slope of the hill in the direction of the distant tower. Standing behind it, a sly grin formed on the boy's face.

"TALON, I order you to use your vibration ability to attract that herd of Triceratops over here!"

"Master?"

"Don't argue!" whispered the boy under his breath. "I want rid of this robot!"

Knowing that its master was now under the control of his evil side, TALON hesitated for a moment, then realised that getting rid of the robot was a sensible step. Once alone with James, TALON might find a way to snap him out of his rage-induced dark side.

Vibrating at a particular frequency, the tiny device focused its sonic beam tightly at the herd of dinosaurs. In the distance they stirred, then snorted and turned in the direction of the hill.

"Wait!" shouted James at the robot. "I need the toilet. Despite the urgency of the situation I need to relieve myself before continuing on the quest. It's alright for you robots; you don't have this problem! Time travel does not seem to affect normal bodily functions, so even though I might have been away from home only minutes, the hours I spend on the mission take their toll on my body."

The robot stopped and waited; not bothering to look back "Be quick, boy."

Walking over to a nearby bush James was glad that Max had found time and a way to cut a fly in the molecule flexible metal suit! The living computer had not been completely deceitful.

Still attached to James's belt, TALON whispered to its master. "The herd are on their way. I have found a sonic pitch which really irritates them. It is at a pitch too low for humans, or that robot to hear. However the dinosaurs *can* hear it so clearly that it hurts them. They are coming to stop the pain, by stamping out the noise."

"Hold on to your hat, TALON... We are about to make a last second *location jump* over to that distant tower!"

"But I don't wear a hat, Master..."

"Just an old-fashioned phrase, TALON. Now put a curtain of barrier sound around the robot, so it cannot detect the approach of the beasts until it is too late. Then project the source of the irritating noise onto the robot."

The small sphere chuckled when it realised what its master was planning. "The robot is going to get flattened by the herd!"

"Yes; absolutely, completely and utterly stomped into the ground!" smirked James slyly.

"And with it out of the way I can get rid of this collar, get the crystal and use it for myself," he boasted.

Suddenly the upper half of the robot rotated around to face him, while the lower half remained pointing down the hill. "What are you up to, boy?"

"Having a *Pee…*"

"P?" it responded.

James turned and faced the metallic figure. "Yes *P* for; I *predict* that you are in *peril*. And are about to be *painfully punished* by being *pounced-on, pinned-down, pummelled,* and *pulped.* In a nutshell P for *perish…*"

The robot's arms rose in alarm and numerous weapons began to extend out them. However a second later the herd of triceratops burst into view from the surrounding trees and swarmed onto the hapless robot. The roar of the beasts echoed through the hills, drowning out the sound of metal being crushed under massive clawed feet.

At the same moment James and TALON location jumped out of the way.

*

In the cell, the alien leader was continuing to flaunt its power over Max and Davius.

"The boy will do what we say. Once he has got all the crystals for us we *will* take over the world. We will use the twelve Dark Zodiac clones to rule on our behalf, while we concentrate on putting humans into camps. Some be selected for food while others are converted into slaves and shock troops. Once the earth has been transformed into the type

93

of world we want, we will set about rebuilding our space empire."

Max hovered in the far side of the cell, refusing to be taunted by its rival. Instead its complex internal living circuitry was frantically exploring how to bring its weapons back on-line.

Davius slowly paced around the cell, stroking his beard thoughtfully. "I still find all this fantastic. Max is from a race called the Metvals and you are rival aliens called the Zentoria."

He shook his head in amazement. "It has taken me this long to accept that there are other races in space and that they are not sky-gods. To now find that there was a long war between Metvals and Zentoria is amazing."

Keeping his other thoughts to himself he realised that to have witnessed Atlantis at its height was also amazing. The wise old man now wondered who the Atlantians had been and where they had come from!

Chapter 21

Mary continued to crawl along the air pipe as quickly as she could. She was desperate to put as much distance between her and the grilled opening as possible. All the while the air being sucked through the pipe was getting warmer and the animal smells getting stronger. After pausing for breath she pressed on, until she came to a T-junction. Twisting dark pipes stretched in each direction; however she could just make out a faint green glow from the one on the right. Hoping that it might be a way out, she twisted her aching body and crawled in that direction.

She wished that one of her boy friends was here to protect her; then changed her mind, remembering that they were all pretty puny. That's why she was able to boss them about so easily.

Reluctantly she wished that her parents were here to help her. They might be old nags but she now realised how much she took them for granted. But James was different; it was his fault that she was trapped in this pipe in the first place!

Outside her pipe the alien's base was bathed in an eerie green light which ebbed and flowed from the organic looking brown walls. The sound of flowing liquid reverberated throughout the strange structure like a moaning voice. Even the solid looking walls seemed alive in some unnatural way.

Inside the pipe she finally reached the source of the green glow and stopped. The elbows of her top and the knees of her tights had worn through, from rubbing up against the metal of the pipe. She needed to get out of it before her skin was scratched away as well!

This time the opening was different. It did not have a grill and was as big as the pipe. It had several metal lumps sticking out around the edge of the opening, like some strange welding that had left solid finger-shaped blobs on the join. Looking out through the opening she saw a massive chamber containing a huge transparent tank shaped like a rugby ball. The tank was brimming with swirling, transparent green ooze. Her pipe was on the side furthest away from the tank and seemed to be partly embedded in the chamber's organic wall. Looking out again, she noticed that there was a walkway about four metres below the pipe. She cursed under her breath; it was too far to jump.

Then she had a brainwave. Twisting around in the uncomfortably small pipe, she brought her knees up to her chest and quickly took off her boots. Then squirming around and rolling onto her back she pulled off her tights. Having completed that awkward manoeuvre she put her boots back on; turned over and crawled back to the opening.

Tying one end of the tights to a finger-shaped metal blob in the pipe's opening, she threw the other end outside.

She hoped that there were not too many holes in them. She wanted to lower herself safely onto the walkway, not fall and be killed!

*

James always found the sensation of location jumps very different from time travel.

Simply moving from one location to another in the same time period was like being in the centre of a swirling vortex of a silent storm. Except that he was surrounded by twisting and turning black and white images. It was like looking at an old silent film his great grandparents might have watched when they were his age.

He suddenly appeared out of thin air on the top of the tower; and crouched down to avoid being seen.

The tower was like a very tall lighthouse constructed out of carefully cut curved blocks of stone.

Just like an old-style lighthouse, it had a flat top and a wider observation area where a light would normally be. Instead of glass sides, the observation area had wide open spaces. The blocks forming the building were finely cut and constructed so tightly that even a slip of paper could not have been slid between the joins. He scratched the top of his head with confusion. Who could have built such a thing?

Looking up, he saw that the glow of the asteroid was now high in the sky above the tower. It was definitely getting bigger and closer; and seemed to be lining up with the tower!

He needed to get inside the tower, overcome the guardian, find the crystal and get away as soon as possible!

"TALON, the Sagittarius symbol is half man, half horse. Do you know what the guardian will look like?"

"No, Master, but I detect movement in the base of the tower; which seems to be climbing stairs inside. I suggest you find the crystal before whoever it is gets to the top!"

Without the survival kit from his back pack, James had no way of climbing down; so he would have to risk a location jump down into the confines of the tower. Concentrating, he closed his eyes, pushed the controls on his wrist and vanished.

A second later he appeared in the observation area.

Opening one eye, then both, he looked around the circular room. The stone walls were carved with a detailed picture of landscapes and dinosaurs. In the centre there was a circular stone column just over a metre high and a metre wide. All over it were carved strange images of creatures which appeared to be half human. Sitting on top of the column was the Sagittarius crystal. It was as TALON's records described. The last of the three fire sign crystals was egg sized, rounded, its Turquoise glow heightening its light blue surface and the glittering green streaks which ran through it.

His evil side smiled with satisfaction. Soon he would have the power to do whatever he wanted!

Now they were close to it James and TALON could feel its throbbing power.

"TALON, why couldn't we detect its intense energy when we were outside?"

"Because all its power seems to be focused onto a small point in the sky, Master."

"The asteroid!" gasped James. "It's being used to attract the asteroid!"

Suddenly James heard noises behind him and he span around to face them.

The scraping sound was being caused by a concealed door sliding open in the wall; and in the passage outside he could hear hissing and heavy breathing.

Instinctively James pulled his suit's collapsible breathing helmet out of its collar and over his head. Throwing himself against the far wall he activated the suit's camouflage ability; and it automatically blended with the wall. From head to toe he could not be seen. Suddenly he gasped, realising that his belt and TALON were still visible!

He could hear the sounds getting closer; whatever was outside was about to enter the room.

His fingers fumbling, he unclipped the belt and tucked it up behind him; against the wall out of sight.

Suddenly several figures strode into the room.

Looking up James saw three creatures; each half human and half dinosaur!

Eyes bulging with fear, he stifled a gasp of horror as they turned to face him!

*

James's parents went about their business as usual until one of James's friends called on the phone; trying to contact him. It was still the school holidays and they had hardly seen him!

She had thought that James was with his friends, and assured him that James was not at home.

Once Christine had switched the phone off she sat down and tried to imagine where her son was. It was strange, but a fog of confusion seemed to cloud her memory. Even though she did not know where James was; for some strange reason she did not feel concerned!

Just then the phone rang again, and Mary's boyfriend (well the one she was seeing this week) was calling after her; she too was missing! After telling him that Mary was also "out", she hung up and put her head in her hands. Only days ago she and Alan had been having furious rows with her about smoking, drinking and boys; but now they did not seem concerned about their daughter! Not only that, but she and her husband had also been arguing with each other so much that the marriage was under threat. Now it was as if she and her husband had undergone a transformation; not least no longer thinking about James and Mary. It was as if a section of their memory had been erased.

Little did she realise that Max had doused them in its amnesia ray; wiping out memories of the previous Dark Zodiac attack on them. It had also removed any of their curiosity or concerns about James.

She sighed and stood up, not too bothered about the phone calls, and got on with her work.

Chapter 22

The human-dinosaurs looked around the chamber suspiciously. Pressed against the wall as tightly as possible, James dared not breathe. He was convinced that one of the creatures was looking directly at him!

After a moment they shook their heads and turned their attention to the crystal.

"I thought that I could smell something unusual," said one with a hiss.

"And I thought that I could hear something close by," said another with a higher pitched hiss.

The third creature, which was slightly taller and more muscular, shook its head.

"Go back down to the bottom of the tower and stand guard while I activate the crystal."

James tried to slow his panting as best he could, for fear of being heard. His heart was also pounding like a fast drum at the base of his throat. He hoped that it could not be heard by them. His body was also sweating with fear, causing trickles to run down the inside of his time suit. He was glad that it was airtight; and the breathing helmet was sealing his odour in. At least the creatures would not be able to smell him. He had always thought that his camouflage suit would make him undetectable, now he realised that opponents could track him down using their other senses!

"Seal the entrance behind you," ordered the tallest creature as the other two strode out of the chamber.

Despite the fear he felt, James could still marvel at the way his suit was able to translate the local language of wherever he went into modern English.

Calming down, he began to study the creature. It was almost three metres tall, with mottled, scaly skin. It was a cross between a humanoid shape, and an upright dinosaur (like a T-Rex), with a ground-length tail. The creature was obviously advanced, as it was wearing gold bracelets around its wrists and ankles. It also had a gold breastplate, with the Sagittarius astrology symbol embossed into it.

He knew the Sagittarius symbol was of a creature half man and half horse. What it really meant was half human and half animal! This was the guardian of the crystal.

The creature positioned itself in front of the circular stone column; its head higher than the crystal balanced on its flat top.

It stretched out its arms and touched the crystal with both of its clawed hands. Immediately a circular hole began to open in the roof of the chamber and the crystal began to crackle with energy.

Looking up James could see the approaching asteroid through the hole.

The crystal began to hiss loudly, sounding like a food on a barbecue. The more it hissed, the hotter it grew.

The heat began to fill the chamber, attacking the walls and the skin of his time suit!

Automatically the suit responded to the temperature change and cooled his body in equal measure; James just hoped that it could cope with the sudden assault.

Looking into the centre of the chamber he saw that the creature was impervious to the crystal's heat; protected by an energy field extending from the column.

Looking up through the hole, James saw that the asteroid was beginning to veer slightly to one side. The power of the crystal was enormous; it was deflecting it away from the earth! This must not be allowed to happen. The gigantic rock was supposed to smash into the earth, causing the extinction of the dinosaurs!

Whoever this intelligent race of reptiles was; they too were supposed to be destroyed in the extinction event. So totally wiped out that not even their fossil remains would survive!

In his mission to get the first fire crystal he had reluctantly allowed Mount Vesuvius to erupt and destroy Pompeii and Herculaneum. He was stronger willed now, and had unleashed his darker personality. He could easily do it again!

Taking a deep breath, he slowly began to slide along the wall, moving around behind the creature. But how could he overcome it? He did not have another crystal to use, nor did he have any weapons.

Now closer to the creature, he could see its blood red eyes and razor sharp teeth. It may be the leader of an intelligent race of reptiles; but it was still a super-powered monster compared to him!

Reaching behind his back, James tapped twice on TALON, as a signal. Taking its cue, TALON began to vibrate very fast and make a high-pitched whine.

The Sagittarius guardian suddenly roared out load and dropped the crystal; clasping its claws to its head.

The crystal landed near James, and he knelt down to pick it up. The creature was now rolling around on the floor hissing and roaring furiously, unable to stop James.

"Well done for using your sonic defence systems," said James as he quickly strapped his belt back on.

"Not so fast, intruder!" screeched the creature and it sprang to its feet, fighting off the pain of TALON's sonic attack.

Suddenly any trace of culture vanished from the creature and it stood opposite him, poised to pounce. Its eyes blazed like fire, saliva dribbled from its jaws and its teeth were fully bared!

"I'll save you, Master!" screamed TALON and it vibrated even faster and began to wobble. For a moment it looked as if the little metal ball was going to fall out of its belt pouch and onto the floor. Instead it popped out, floated up and stopped in mid air!

"I forgot you can fly now!" exclaimed the boy with relief.

"Not fly well, but I can hover at low heights for short periods, by vibrating my armoured shell at a particular level," it responded.

However the creature was not impressed and sprang at them. Despite the pain, it was not going to be defeated by the stranger's technology. "I will slice you up alive, soft skin!" Lashing out it swatted TALON aside like a fly. The little metal sphere was sent flying out of the window space, uttering a high-pitched scream. The creature landed next to James and snapped at him with its slavering jaws. Desperately the boy leapt to one side and pressed himself against the wall, hoping that his camouflaged suit would hide him again!

"Not this time, intruder!"

It sprang directly at him and grabbed him by the throat. "I may not be able to see you properly, but I can smell and hear you!"

Without effort it squeezed his neck hard and lifted him off the floor; his feet dangling like a puppet's.

"I don't know what you are; you don't smell like a reptile or insect. But once I have used the crystal to deflect the asteroid, you will make an interesting raw meal."

Chapter 23

The aliens separated Max and Davius, intending to question them while James was away on his mission. It was the leader's intention to interrogate Max and Davius for different information about James. Since the boy had destroyed the Dark Zodiac's own base, all knowledge about him had been lost. The leader knew that if it was going to successfully control the boy it had to know as much as possible about him!

Max remained in the same cell, while Davius was forced to march to an identical one on the opposite side of the control room.

The leader remained in the cell with Max, while its deputy hovered in front of Davius in the other cell.

It was going to be a battle of wills, if James Lightwater's details were going to remain secret!

*

Holding on so strong that her knuckles were turning white, Mary had managed to lower herself as far as she could with her tights. Looking down she saw that she still had two metres to go. Suddenly the tights tore loudly! With a gasp she fell onto the walkway, landing on her bottom with a meaty smack.

Biting her lip, she kept her painful scream silent, desperate not to attract attention.

Her bottom was going to sting for ages and she blamed her useless brother!

Looking around, she could not see any robots. Determined not to be discovered she quickly knelt down to make sure that her boots were done up tightly.

Standing up she looked along the walkway in each direction; the structure curled around the wall of the chamber. However across the other side of the chamber she could see a circular entrance in the wall, joining the walkway. She set off towards it at a brisk, but quiet pace.

It was as she neared the hole, that she looked back towards the huge circular tank and saw something inside it. She had assumed that it was some sort of water storage tank, but now she realised with horror that it was keeping things alive!

Inside the strange swirling liquid were swimming several large jelly fish-like creatures.

Several of them suddenly glowed with a deep purple light and went motionless, their thoughts being transmitted to one another. With a hum, a large transparent sphere (like a giant goldfish bowl, Mary thought), descended from metal openings in the ceiling of the chamber and entered the liquid. To her amazement, the sphere floated down and one of the jelly fish-like creatures swam into an opening in its base. The opening then closed, the sphere floated back to the surface and then flew into the air.

Suppressing a terrified scream, she ran along the walk way and through the dark hole. The robots were bad enough, but these creatures were hideous she thought!

As she emerged into the next room, she was confronted by something so horrible that everything she had experienced so far was nothing in comparison.

*

The force of the dinosaur-creature's swipe had sent TALON hurtling out of the window like a rocket. However now airborne, it had easily raised its level of vibration and instead of smashing into the ground it had come to a controlled hover.

TALON was only a few hundred metres from the base of the tower and could detect a perimeter of low outbuildings, protected by several dozen of the reptile-creatures.

Extending its scanning range it detected the not-too-distant herd of triceratops. "Master will be grateful that I have found the sonic pitch which really irritates them. It will confuse the towers creatures and attract the herd once again to come and stamp out the noise!"

*

In the tower the creature was looking for some way to secure James, so it could go back to the crystal. Its first task was to use the crystal, then once it had turned the asteroid away from the earth, it would feast on James!

Suddenly they were aware of a violent vibrating from TALON and felt the sharp stab of pain as it zoomed in through the window. Once again TALON was proving to be far more than a know-it-all tracking device, thought James. Perhaps James would not destroy it once he had got all the crystals!

The dinosaur-creature roared loudly and dropped James so it could cover its head with its claws. Foam spraying from its jaws, its lips curled back to expose rows of razor sharp teeth.

"Grab the crystal and location jump out of here!" barked TALON with a surprisingly assertive electronic voice.

Struggling to protect himself from the noise, the boy staggered forward and snatched up the crystal with both hands.

Looking up through the opening in the roof he could see the asteroid thundering down towards them.

Suddenly the herd of triceratops outside smashed into the base of the tower causing it to shudder.

"I invited some friends of ours, Master!"

Outside they could hear the dinosaur-creatures being trampled by the triceratops. Next there were loud crashes and walls began to buckle. "I have centred the sonic signal on myself, Master. While I am in the tower they will continue to attack it."

Suddenly the floor of the chamber gave way and James fell into the mass of collapsing masonry.

Desperately TALON managed to cartwheel out of the window before the roof fell in.

James hit the bottom of the hollow tower with full force; his time suit absorbing most of the violent impact. A large piece of masonry narrowly missed his head and crashed into the rubble-strewn floor next to him.

Shaking his head to clear it, he looked up and shouted in horror as he saw the whole of the building was collapsing in on him! TALON's plan had worked too well! Without time to think, he pulled the crystal close into his chest and curled himself into a tight ball. Cringing with fear, he screwed his eyes up tight and waited for the impact of the tons of rubble.

Chapter 24

Mary had entered a nightmare. The exit from the chamber with the flying jelly fish led into a smaller room. It was dimly lit by red glowing orbs which protruded from the ceiling. It was a long, thin room filled with equipment which reminded her of a hospital ward. However its walls were curved and organic, resembling the bones of a giant ribcage. The room was hot and smelled foul. Along each ribbed wall she saw attached a series of coffin-sized glass containers. For a moment she thought that they contained more of the strange bandaged beings she had seen earlier; but she was wrong!

These glass coffins contained people! Each one stared out with blank expressions, their breath forming condensation on the inside of the glass. Shuddering with fear she began to back away towards the door she had entered by. Suddenly there was a noise behind her and without turning to look she threw herself to one side. She landed with a thump behind some metal containers; and rolled out of sight. Looking up she saw one of the giant goldfish bowls, with a jelly fish creature inside, glide into the room.

The creature steered the travel sphere down the centre of the long room then stopped opposite one of the glass containers. The being inside twisted its tentacles with excitement and operated some controls in the base of the hovering sphere. Out of the sphere extended a plastic tube, which Mary thought looked like a transparent garden hose pipe. The metallic end of the tube slotted into a hole in the bottom of the glass container; containing a man.

Mary looked closer to see what was happening. Red liquid began to flow through the tube from the man's glass container into the hovering travel sphere!

Mary turned away in horror and put her hands over her mouth. These creatures were eating people!

Overtaken by sheer panic she leapt up and ran out of the room.

The creature in the sphere did not notice her, as it was completely absorbed in its meal. However the spy camera in the chamber did see her and began to follow her movements!

*

The alien leader floated around the cell, exchanging thoughts with Max.

"So we meet face to face at last," it said with an accusing tone. "We Zentoria were chasing your Metval star ship to finish off your race. There had to be an end to such a long war. The war has reduced our two races to near extinction."

Max knew the Zentoria were a dying race and there were only a few of them left. So few of them that they were not able to conquer the earth by themselves. That is why they had made secret alliances with corrupt members of Earth's Governments and create the Dark Zodiac.

Max also knew that the Zentoria had been scheming to take over the Earth; needing humans for food and to re-build their slave-armies. Their own planet had died long ago. They only had one star craft left and for centuries they had been searching for a suitable world to colonise.

However Max had been amazed when the Zentoria had uncovered a period of Earth history which had long since been forgotten by humans. An Atlantian civilisation once powered by twelve zodiac crystals. However, Max knew that the Zentorians couldn't go after the crystals themselves. Unlike Max, their bodies could not withstand the physical pressures of time travel! That is why they had to design the time craft for the Dark Zodiac to use on their behalf.

Max mused to itself. It may be trapped by its rivals but its knowledge still gave it an advantage. What it did regret bitterly, was its need to deceive James. Perhaps it should have told him the truth from the start?

The alien floated around Max, impatiently trying to provoke a response from its rival. "We calculated that there may have been a sole survivor from the Metval craft which crashed here on Earth. But we never guessed that it was you Maximus-Prime!"

The green sphere finally acknowledged the Zentoria's presence and rotated itself to face its rival.

"You are correct. Once I had crash landed, I set about building my own base in secret. Unlike you I avoided all contact with humans. Over the years I secretly monitored your activities and your agreements with the human conspirators. I could not believe how gullible some humans were, or how quickly some were prepared to betray their own kind!

"You are also correct; eventually I learned of your plans to get the crystals and rebuild your race. However as soon as I saw the messages on the stone tablet I knew that you could also be stopped. Not by me, but by the boy!"

The Zentoria's tentacles writhed in excitement, slapping up against the inside of the transparent bubble; stirring the liquid around it.

"So you admit that you intercepted our secret messages about the stone tablet and the coin!"

"Of course I do. My brain is superior to yours. I de-coded the messages and using my superior intelligence I interpreted the meaning of the tablet. This helped me to identify who the boy referred to on it was. I was also able to construct TALON to decrypt the locations on the coin.

"But I knew that I needed to force the boy to go on the quest without giving away who I was, or my true motives."

What Max knew but the aliens did not, was that James was a descendant of ancient Atlantis. Nor did they know the true importance of Davius, as a descendant of the leaders of ancient Atlantis! Above all it must not reveal to the aliens that the three of them had been there. Nor that they had also seen the future!

The alien floated closer to Max. "So you admit that whatever you told the boy was a complete pack of lies!"

Max narrowed its eye, as if in shame. "That is true. Only now I wish that I had been honest with him from the start. Now I know him better, I realise that he is a good person and would have helped me anyway."

The alien quivered with excitement. "Your scheme's backfired! Your have driven him to the evil side of the crystals' influence! He is on our side now..."

*

TALON hovered over the pile of collapsed masonry, flying in and out of the swirling dust. By now the triceratopses were charging away from the remains of the tower, as TALON had switched off its vibrations signal. The herd had done its job well; too well. Far from scattering the reptile-creatures, they had completely destroyed the tower and the township!

It floated over the mounds of rubble scanning for signs of life. Even if its master had become evil; it did not want him to die. Meanwhile high in the sky the asteroid burned even brighter as it began to enter Earth's outer atmosphere.

Suddenly a section of the tower's rubble lying on the ground; exploded skywards and James sprang out. Somersaulting dramatically, he landed expertly on an area of pavement away from the tower base.

"The crystal shielded you, Master!"

The boy stood still, holding the crystal in both hands. Sparks of electricity and flickers of flame darted around him like living things.

"Its power is incredible. I can feel pure fire building up inside me. Once I combine this with the five crystals I already have, I will be invincible! Nothing will be able to stop me taking over the world for myself!"

Suddenly he began to twist and jerk wildly. TALON floated closer and scanned him, sensing what was happening. It was as if he was fighting the power of the crystal!

Like all humans James may have a dark and nasty side; but TALON knew humans also had a good side. Now such raw crystal power was filling his entire body. Filling it so completely that there would only be room for good or evil; not both!

The air of this prehistoric world was suddenly shattered by a terrible scream. James dropped the crystal and held his head in his hands, his face twisted and contorted into a hideous shape. Tears streaming down his face, he fell to his knees crying, no human frame could contain such power.

The crystal span around on the ground and began to shake wildly; sparks and flames spitting from it. The boy's mind was locked in a battle of wills with its incredible power.

His wild eyes rolled around madly and he began to dribble. His body began to shake faster and faster. Then with a deep animal groan James slumped to the ground exhausted.

For a moment, the only sound TALON could hear was the wind and the call of distant flying dinosaurs. Then abruptly James came to and raised himself up to a sitting position.

"It's over, the evil side of my personality has been driven out for ever," he gasped.

"Have faith in your skills, Master," urged TALON. "It is you who controls the crystals, not the other way around."

The tracker floated down close to him and landed in his lap. James patted it affectionately. "You saved my life, little friend."

The small ball hummed excitedly. "One more thing I can do for you, Master, if you will sit upright for me."

Without questioning, the boy sat up and waited. Next TALON hummed again and the control collar which James was wearing snapped open and fell to the ground.

"Thank you."

Feeling much better he leaned forward, picked up the crystal and placed it in one of his belt pouches. Next he put TALON safely onto the ground and stood up.

Turning, he looked up and saw the huge asteroid was beginning to fill the sky.

"Impact is only minutes' away, Master."

"Sorry to leave you," responded James, "But I have to go now!"

With that the boy time burst away, leaving the tracker alone in the growing shadow of the asteroid.

"Come back!" yelled TALON, stunned to be abandoned by its master.

Chapter 25

Mary fled panic-stricken along a winding corridor, too frightened to stop and look behind her! What sort of nightmare was her brother involved in? Ahead of her the corridor curved to the left as if it was going in a giant circle. It was dimly lit by an eerie green glow. Suddenly one of the flying transparent spheres floated into view ahead of her; rushing towards her! Screaming out loud, she skidded to a halt and stood transfixed; her eyes wide open with terror. Whatever these things were she wasn't going to give in without a fight! It would have to chase her back through the maze of passages first!

She turned and came face to face with another transparent sphere hovering silently behind her! Before she could scream it fired a jet of green liquid at her. It struck her in the face and smothered her screams; leaving only her nose free to breathe. From behind, the other sphere fired several jets and she was plastered head to toe in the alien ooze. Helpless she toppled sideways and fell onto the floor with a thud. She lay there wide-eyed, but unable to move or speak.

"Take her for interrogation," said one of the creatures. In response the other projected a purple energy beam from the base of its sphere and her wriggling shape floated helplessly into the air. Suddenly the sphere whooshed along the corridor and she was pulled along behind it in the purple light. All she was aware of was the two aliens' thoughts in her head, discussing what they were going to do with her!

*

James hated to leave TALON alone to his fate, but he knew that the aliens were able to track it, whenever it travelled through time. Likewise they could track the control collar. James's quick thinking had made him leave both behind!

He had decided that before he returned to the alien's base, he was going home to get the other five crystals. This madness had to end! Now he was back in control of his senses, he was going to use all his crystals to wipe out the aliens once and for all!

Finally he felt confident that he could control all the crystals.

Suddenly he emerged from the swirling vortex of time travel and landed in the cellar beneath his parents' house. Without hesitation he strode across the room and removed the crystals from the Horoscope Matrix.

Next he clipped on another belt, which had lots of pouches and put a crystal in each. With everything secured, he stood in the centre of the room, activated his wrist control and vanished in a swirl of rainbow light.

*

At last Davius was alone in the cell! For some unexplained reason the aliens' deputy leader had been called away to an emergency. He had to seize this opportunity to be alone while he could!

He just wished he had time to dwell on his new past as a descendant of Atlantis. It was an amazing revelation that his ancestors and James's ancestors had lived in Atlantis and known each other!

This made the messages on the stone tablet even more complex and important. It also meant that it was even less of a coincidence that Maximus-Prime had contacted James and that his first mission brought James and Davius together! If they all escaped from this mess, it would put a whole new direction into the quest.

However he must put those thoughts aside for now. He must exploit this unexpected moment while he was alone and try to focus his powers. He was an expert at tapping into earth energy in the British Isles. He was even able to project his image and powers across time for brief periods, but being trapped in an alien base on the far side of the world was new to him.

He took a deep breath and sat down cross-legged in the centre of the cell. He folded his arms across his chest and closed his eyes. Lifting his head back he began to breathe deeply and slowly. He knew that the network of energy lines which he could tap into, criss-crossed the British Isles and beyond. But did they extend as far as Easter Island?

What he had once called magic, Davius now knew was science. But whatever his abilities were called, Davius now extended his focused thoughts in all directions. The first thing he could sense were the strange powers of the aliens' equipment trying to block his thoughts. Concentrating, he got past them by visualising pushing their barriers aside. Next he stretched his mind beyond the base and beyond the island. In his mind he could see a vast ocean in all directions. But by extending his mind's power through it, he could sense the energy lines. The harder he concentrated the clearer the invisible network of earth energy became; like a vast spider's web covering the whole planet!

Suddenly his body jerked as if he had touched a live electric wire. He had succeeded in reaching the energy! Taking a deep breath of satisfaction, his lips formed into a thin, cunning smile.

*

"That boy's abandoned me!" cursed TALON at the top of its electronic voice. The shadow cast by the asteroid now spread across the prehistoric landscape like a huge oil slick. There were only seconds left to go before the extinction event happened!

"The brat must have lied and still be under the influence of his evil side!"

It vibrated with fury and sent out wild bursts of electronic chatter and high-pitched curses. "I knew I couldn't trust him. This is typical of how unreliable he is!"

Suddenly James appeared out of mid air next to TALON. In one smooth move he snatched up both the tracker and the control collar and then vanished again.

"I had every confidence in you, at all times, Master..." said TALON sheepishly.

Seconds later the asteroid struck the earth with an impact of several million nuclear weapons. The resulting impact blasted vast amounts of material into the atmosphere blotting out the sun and spreading radiation across much of the earth. The ground heaves and contorts like liquid, creating a crater more than 180 kilometres in diameter. A storm of fire sweeps across the planet's surface scorching out of existence most life in the area. The dinosaurs and other creatures die out. And all traces of the lizard race are incinerated. Erasing the alternative line of intelligent life from the world forever; leaving the way open for humans to evolve.

Millions of years later the location would be called the Chicxulub crater in the Yucatan Peninsula, Mexico. But no one would ever know what James had done; allowing the extinction of an alternative earthly race...

Chapter 26

Mary came to, feeling groggy. She had passed out soon after she had been captured. However she suddenly became aware of feeling stretched in all directions! Opening her eyes she realised that she was spread-eagled inside a large metal ring! The ring was several metres in diameter and stretched her absolutely taut. The ring was floating upright, a metre above the floor in a metal-walled room. Two of the aliens were hovering close by and two shiny metallic robots stood guard over the closed door. One of the aliens was the deputy leader; called away from questioning Davius!

Mary then noticed that the strange goo was no longer coating her body. Her clothes were wet where the mixture had been pressure-washed off.

She tried to call out but she couldn't! Panicking, she began to struggle; but her hands and feet were held tight by metal cuffs on her wrists and ankles. However no chains connected the cuffs to the large metal ring! She pulled against the ring again but found that her hands and feet could not move at all. The metal cuffs must be held to the ring by magnetism!

She tried to shake her head and cry out again but found that a similar metal and plastic strip had been placed in her mouth and fastened at the back of her neck!

She could also feel a round object in her mouth, attached to the ring. Much as she tried to shout, absolutely nothing came out…

Suddenly one of the aliens projected its thoughts into her head.

"There is no point struggling. The device in your mouth is electronic. It absorbs all sound at its source. The face strip is magnetic and holds your head motionless against the interrogation ring. The wrist and ankle restraints are also electromagnetic; holding you within the ring without the need for cables or chains."

Suddenly the other alien spoke to its colleague, its voice echoing in Mary's head.

"Time is short. We need to know who she is and how she got here. Use the mind probe!"

Mary heard a low electric hum above her and a face-sized electronic device was lowered in front of her from the ceiling. It was shaped like a full face mask made of metal and plastic, except that it had no eye holes. It hung from a thin metal bar, which allowed it to rise or fall from its compartment in the ceiling. Suddenly it glowed brightly and began to hum. Then one of the aliens used a thought command to move it towards her, covering her face. She screamed silently.

*

The alien leader circled Max again; trying to scan and probe its complex inner brain; but the ugly green ball simply floated motionless. In frustration the alien thrashed about inside its travel sphere, swirling the liquid around it. The Zentoria were not used to having their incredible minds being blocked! Bitterly the creature remembered how advanced the Metvals were. It would take specialist equipment to get the information out of Maximus-Prime!

Suddenly a wide door slid open in the side of the cell and another alien floated in.

"I bring a message from your deputy, he is interrogating another intruder."

Before the leader could respond another alien floated in and stopped alongside the first messenger. "Leader, I urgently report that the boy has made a time burst. We are tracking the TALON and the control collar; they are returning here!"

The leader turned and faced Max excitedly. "You see, I told you! The boy has completed his mission and is bringing the crystal to me. He is on our side!"

Max said nothing, its artificial skin remaining silent. The living computer still refused to acknowledge that James was on the side of the enemy. It could not face the idea that its deceptions had driven the boy over the edge and into the arms of the aliens!

The leader rotated around to face its two colleagues. "Move everyone back into the main control chamber and prepare to greet the boy. Our success begins here!"

*

James enjoyed the warm comfort of the strange place – between worlds during time bursts. Even though the physics of time travel told him he was only travelling through the time vortex for a few seconds; it always felt as if it was much longer. He had time to think clearly, forget his less-than-happy home life and escape from the pressures of the quest!

And then he felt it. The tug at his body and spirit which told him that he was about to land back in the alien base.

Without further warning he emerged from the time vortex and stepped onto the floor as confidently as if he was stepping off an escalator!

He felt calm and confident. He had enough crystals to free his friends and blast the aliens out of existence. His plan was simple. No complicated schemes, just blasting and escaping!

The main chamber was lit by a combination of eerie green spheres and spotlights.

Ten aliens floated in a line in front of him; all in transparent travel spheres. The leader floated slightly nearer. On his left sat Max, suspended slightly above the floor. It was held in a spherical cage not much wider than its body. The bars of the cage were made of flickering electricity. Sat on the floor on the other side of the alien, Davius was imprisoned in a similar electrical cage.

"Welcome, my friend…" said the alien leader in a confident voice which echoed around the chamber.

Suddenly alarms sounded and James was caught in a brilliant spotlight shining down from the ceiling.

The leader stopped and scanned the boy, then floated back a few metres.

"So you were trying to deceive me, boy. My instruments detect that you are no longer wearing the control collar."

James smirked and nodded, realising that he had lost the element of surprise, but confident that he had the power to win the imminent battle.

"Not only that, but I am completely free of the dark influence of the crystals. I am in complete control now!" he shouted. Next he tossed the control collar across the room contemptuously, to land on the floor near the alien. Then he held up TALON in his other hand, as if taunting the aliens.

Hearing that James was himself again, Davius nodded in relief and began to focus his mind on the energy lines he had connected with while alone in his cell. He must seize the moment as the aliens were now completely concentrating on James, and ignoring him. This was the moment to clear his mind and tap into that earth energy!

The alien leader continued to scan the boy and then suddenly recoiled in fear.

"The boy has six crystals on him! He has six crystals!"

Max's big red eye opened wide with a jerk as it realised that James had the crystals. The boy had made the ultimate gamble; bringing them here could let them fall into the aliens' control and the quest would be over! Detecting that the aliens and robots were concentrating on James, it scanned around the chamber. Desperately it analysed Davius's strange brain patterns, and concluded with alarm that the old man was slipping into a deep coma. There was nothing left but for Max to activate its internal self-destruct mechanism. The crystals must not fall into its rival's clutches!

Concentrating on the alien leader, James stepped forward confidently and pointed at his belt. In response the belt's pouches began to glow; as the crystals inside began to power-up.

"I control these, and they are about to wipe out, you, your human traitors and robots."

In response the alien leader floated forward again, this time as equally confident as James.

"Not so human!"

"Why not… alien!"

"Because we have captured your sister. She was caught in your time vortex and brought here by accident. Our mind probes have given us a lot of information about you!"

James froze in confusion. Was the alien telling the truth?

Before he could act, Mary floated into view behind the row of aliens.

She was spread-eagled inside a large metal ring several metres across. The ring was hovering upright a metre above the floor, with one shiny metallic robot standing guard on each side as it floated forward. Looking closer he saw that the metal cuffs on her wrists, ankles and mouth must be held to the ring by magnetism! Staring closer he saw the terror in her eyes and the tears rolling down her cheeks. The ring began to hum and stretch her slightly in all directions. He could see her trying to scream, but she could not make a sound.

The alien leader floated higher into the air, asserting its dominance over James.

"Unless you want to see her pulled slowly apart, you will surrender to me!"

James narrowed his eyes and considered if he could get to the ring and use the power of the crystals to fee her. However, the alien continued to block his way and threaten him.

"And before you even think about freeing her, the ring is booby trapped," it laughed. "And if you so much as touch her it will send thousands of volts of electricity through her!"

James sighed and nodded in acceptance of the aliens' demands. The boy reflected that if he had still been under the influence of his evil side, he might have dared to defy the aliens. But his good side was compassionate, and less likely to risk a loved one's life (even if it was his sister).

Reluctantly he surrendered.

Chapter 27

Several robots surrounded James and trained guns on him. Not only did he feel scared, but he felt angry with himself. He should have thought of a better battle plan. His evil side would have! Taking a deep breath he promised to himself that he would get them all out of this mess; and do it without any regrets about banishing his evil personality.

The alien continued to hover high in the chamber; trying to dominate the boy.

"One false move and you will be blasted, boy! I have seen what you can do, when you destroyed ATOSS and the Dark Zodiac's secret base. So you will follow my orders to the letter – or else!"

James nodded in agreement.

"First, boy, you will hand over TALON. If it will not obey us, we will scan it to decode the locations of the remaining crystals."

James held the tracker tightly in one hand; he knew that once he gave up the little ball it would only be able to defend itself for a short while, but the aliens' weapons would eventually overcome it.

"Then you will hand over the six crystals which you are carrying!" continued the alien leader.

James considered this for a moment. If he could focus his thoughts for a few moments he would be able to energise at least one of the crystals. However he knew that the aliens would be watching for him to try this. They would blast him as soon as their instruments detected him disobeying them.

"Then finally you will take off the time suit which you are wearing."

James sniggered to himself. At least the suit would be useless to them. The bond between the suit's material and his skin was unique; created when he was accidentally baited in the energy of the Aquarius crystal and the black time-travel gas. He was the only one able to use it!

However the alien floated lower to view the boy's face more closely.

"Do not grin, boy. We know of the suit's abilities. We are confident that we can adapt it to be used by someone with the same DNA as you. Like your sister!"

James clenched his fists in anger. It had never occurred to him that a close family member may be able to use the suit!

"And then we can kill this meddling boy and use his sister as a slave!" said another alien to the rest of the gathering.

"Yes, use her to get the crystals, rather than risk our new time craft or any of our Dark Zodiac clones!" added another.

James's anger was beginning to rise; however this time without any danger of slipping over to his darker, more dangerous side. It was a gamble, but he had no choice but to risk activating one of the crystals. If only he could do it fast enough!

*

The physical body of the High Priest was still in the aliens' base; however his invisible spirit-form had departed and was now exploring Easter Island. Freed from the limits of his physical form, Davius suddenly found himself floating on the surface of the island. To his amazement he had been able to get past the aliens' electronic defences undetected. They had grown overconfident, now they believed that they had James and all of his companions captured!

Their overconfidence would be their downfall. Davius' ghost-form felt himself drawn across the island, as if a rope was tied to his waist. He must concentrate on activating the energy lines which criss-crossed the world.

Suddenly he saw the rows of mysterious stone statues which had stood on Easter Island for centuries. Their strange, elongated faces seemed to point out to the Pacific Ocean, as if looking for something!

In an instant Davius understood. They were looking out across the planet's surface, each one the point where an energy line converged on the Island!

How utterly stupid the aliens were; hiding their star craft and base here, he thought!

The physical body of Davius suddenly stiffened in its electromagnetic cage; a thin smile curling his lips.

Each statue was like a key. And keys needed to be turned to open doors. Simultaneously he connected with each statue and turned them, opening the flood gates of energy into the island.

On the physical surface of the island all the statues began to twist and turn; breaking away from their foundations. Some rose out of the ground as if a giant underground hand was forcing them up; pushing aside heaps of soil. Pushed up they toppled down the hillside causing great noise and dust. Others simply rotated around and around in their holes, scraping against their rock foundations, causing high-pitched whines which sounded like mysterious beasts howling.

On the invisible level, Davius's actions caused a surge of energy directly into the alien base. Delicate instruments exploded causing a hail of sparks and billowing smoke.

Returning to his physical body, he smiled and hoped that he had done enough to distract the aliens, and given James time to use his crystals!

As soon as the alarms sounded, the remaining aliens automatically rushed to the control chamber. Opening his eyes as he merged with his physical body, Davius saw that in total just fifteen aliens now confronted James! So this was all that remained of the Zentoria race he thought! Fifteen aliens, twelve human clones and a few dozen robots was all that was threatening the earth. The High Priest sat up and watched the boy closely; James must strike with the crystals now!

The alien leader realised that its base was under attack; but it did not know who by. Unable to detect what the High Priest had done, it lashed out at James.

"You and your crystals, boy; I warned you what would happen if you tried to trick me!" it exclaimed and fired a blinding beam of light at him.

Before James could act, the beam struck; knocking him across the floor to land in a dazed heap. The force of the blast knocked TALON out of his hand, and it bounced across the floor. Worse still the buckle on the belt containing the crystals snapped; sending the belt sliding across the floor in a different direction.

Sensing its opportunity the alien floated forward, ready to strike!

*

Max saw that the alien leader was about to get the crystals and powered up its self-destruct mechanism. Thirty seconds to go before detonation! Better that everyone was killed in the explosion rather than the aliens get TALON and the crystals.

Suddenly the energy surge secretly triggered by Davius reached the control chamber. Immediately electrical equipment began to fail, sending sparks and flashes of fire in all directions.

At the same time the electromagnetic cages which imprisoned Max and Davius, flickered and died.

In an instant Max stopped its self-destruct countdown. Before anyone could react, it shot into the air and began to fire at the aliens.

Spinning rapidly back and forward, up and down; it fired blast after blast at the confused aliens, now cowering in their travel spheres. The transparent spheres shattered and exploded, like goldfish bowls cracking and releasing the liquid inside!

Squirming aliens splashed onto the floor amid foaming green liquid; their tentacles thrashing about wildly. A foul stench filled the chamber and the dying creatures uttered high-pitched, haunting cries. Max ignored their helplessness and continued to fire, shooting them where they squirmed helplessly on the floor.

This had to be the final battle between the Metval and the Zentoria! Only one race must win.

Suddenly the remainder of the robots burst into the chamber, guns blazing. Max cartwheeled through the air to avoid their blasts; firing back its own blasts in defence.

Swooping low, it spat from its eye fresh bursts of energy like a machine gun. The remaining robots exploded like tin cans filled with fireworks; scattering bits of metal in all directions. Max may be a living computer, but it had a personality and emotions. It wanted an end to the war with the Zentoria once and for all.

Suddenly it was struck by an energy beam from behind and fell to the floor with a heavy smack.

Slyly, the alien leader floated out from behind its place of hiding and shot at Max again as it lay stunned on the floor.

Groaning, Max ignored its pain, rolled across to James and stopped next to him.

However the boy was still groggy; holding his head with both hands. TALON had also managed to partly recover and roll over to the boy as well.

With a ring of triumph in its voice, the alien leader floated over to them.

Max had little time to act so it used its vibrating skin to talk quickly.

"James, I am sorry that I lied to you. I should have told you the truth from the start. I should have trusted that your decency would have guided your judgement. I should not have used lies to trick you into helping me!"

Feeling groggy, James rolled over and put one hand on Max and the other on TALON.

"Don't worry you ugly, spotty green idiot. We've been through too many battles together and you've saved my life too many times for us to fall out. You are forgiven, my friend; you are forgiven."

For the first time in its existence Max cried. Strange silver liquid formed on its eye and ran out of the corner, dropping onto the floor. James realised with amazement that the living computer had been provoked to tears by human emotion!

"How touching…" smirked the alien leader with contempt, as it closed in on them.

"So the treacherous Maximus-Prime wants forgiveness for its deceit!"

The hideous creature was taunting them, making their final moments alive as miserable as possible.

"Finally I can now take the six crystals and TALON! I may be the last survivor of my race; but with TALON's information, my Dark Zodiac clones, and my time craft, I will get the remaining crystals and still take over the world!

"At last I finally get to personally finish off Maximus-Prime and James Lightwater!" it boomed with triumph!

Chapter 28

The moment the electromagnetic cage had faded from around Davius, he tried to stand. Cringing, he realised that the sheer effort of taking his life force out of his body had completely drained him. Gasping, he fell forward and landed flat on his face. Looking up he saw Max swooping through the air, its blood-red eye firing energy blasts in all directions and winning a great victory. And then it was knocked down from behind by the sly attack from the alien leader. Badly injured, Max rolled across the floor to rest next to James and TALON. Struggling to hear what Max was saying, Davius tried to drag himself forward. Looking up again he saw that Max was crying! How could a living computer shed tears he wondered? It must have a leak instead.

And then the alien leader floated into view and hovered over them menacingly. Davius cursed, the creature was still alive and it was about to get everything it wanted!

He cursed to himself; the quest could not end like this! But the High Priest could do nothing to help. He was exhausted. He had no strength left to put a protective energy field over the boy and his friends. He did not even have the strength to defend himself!

*

As soon as the power to the control chamber had failed, the magnetic field holding Mary in the interrogation ring vanished. Without warning she fell forward onto the floor, only just managing to put her hands out to protect her face from the impact.

Without hesitation she sprang to her feet and stood up. Her wrist and ankle straps were still in place, but no longer worked; however the gag was still fastened at the back of her head. She yelled a string of rude curses, but only a muffled noise could be heard.

All around her, smoke, fire and chaos swirled. Looking up she saw an ugly green ball with a big red eye flying among the smoke. Suddenly it was hit by a flash of light and it fell to the floor and rolled across to rest next to James. Through the smoke and showers of sparks she saw something going on between her brother, the ugly big green ball and a metal cricket ball. A few metres away from them she saw an old man in tatty robes, groaning on the floor.

Frustrated beyond reason she screamed at the top of her voice again; but nothing came out! *She had no idea what was going on, but her fear was rapidly turning into anger!*

And then the last of the horrible, squirming creatures in its giant gold fish bowl flew down and hovered over James.

With a shudder she remembered seeing one of the creatures eating someone earlier on. She felt disgusted. She did not know how her awful brother was involved in all of this, but she had seen enough to know that the creature in the transparent sphere was the enemy.

Suddenly her anger erupted into hate. She screamed louder than ever, this time with terrible rage; and even the gag could not silence her. Her scream echoed around the chamber.

Hearing her, the alien stopped in mid air and rotated in her direction to see what had caused the noise.

Glaring at the alien defiantly, she raised her fists into the air and screamed directly at it. Her anger was even greater and this time the belt of crystals lying on the floor began to glow in response!

An amazed James saw what was happening. "Her anger has activated the crystals. She must have a family connection to them, just like I have!"

Standing bravely in front of the alien she screamed yet again and shook her fists at it. The frustration and terror of her last few hours came bursting out. The belt of crystals glowed even brighter, sending showers of sparks across the floor.

Amazed to see his sister unknowingly activating the crystals, he rolled over and pushed himself onto his knees. Focusing his thoughts on the crystals he closed his eyes and reached out towards the glowing belt. "Crystals to me!"

The belt twitched and span around on the floor several times as if pulled by invisible hands.

"Crystals to me!" he ordered again, this time louder.

Suddenly the belt leapt off the floor and sped through the air towards him.

About to blast Mary, the alien suddenly sensed the belt's movement and stopped. Horror-struck, the alien veered away from James; seeing the crystals glowing into life.

"You won't get me with those, boy! I can still escape with my clones and time craft."

Before anyone could act, the creature whooshed away and out of the chamber through one of the tunnels.

Max rolled alongside James, just as the belt flew into his hand.

"The Zentoria leader is going to escape in some type of atmospheric craft, with the new Dark Zodiac clones and time craft. It must not be allowed to get away."

James tried to stand up, but felt giddy and slumped back down. "But I've got to stop them…"

Max wobbled in frustration on the floor. "No, James, it's too late; we are all too exhausted to do anything else here. And knowing how the Zentoria work, their leader will have activated a massive self-destruct weapon in this base. The aliens cannot afford to let it fall into human hands!"

James shook his head defiantly and tried to get up again.

By now TALON had clicked and hummed into life again. "So, Master, what Maximus-Prime is saying is that this base and the buried star craft which it is built around, are about to go *boom*; and we need to get out of here *now*!"

As James tried to stand up again, his sister came running over to him. She stood there waving her arms about frantically and yelling at the top of her voice, but little sound came out.

"If you ask me, she should wear that gag all the time..." muttered TALON.

"We all need to get out of here and back to the cellar now!" shouted Davius, managing to push himself up into a kneeling position.

James nodded and ordered his sister to help Davius over to them. Exhausted, the old man lent heavily on her as she walked him over to James. As soon as he slumped onto the floor, she tugged on the clasp at the back of her head again in frustration, but it refused to undo. Wild-eyed she stamped her feet in frustration.

Suddenly explosions shook the chamber and bits of the ceiling began to collapse in on the group.

"No time to mess with your gag now, big sis!" barked James, "Quick, everyone get close together on the floor."

Quickly James sat on the floor and positioned himself at the centre of the group. Davius sat on his left and Mary sat on his right, each holding his nearest hand. Mary had Max in her lap and Davius had TALON and the crystals on his. Quickly checking that they were all connected to him, James activated his suit's location jumping ability and they all vanished from the base. Next stop the cellar.

*

On the surface of the Island the statues had stopped moving and everything had returned to normal. Local people and tourists wandered about in confusion, examining the statues to understand what had happened to them.

Seconds later a small, black, saucer-shaped craft shot out of a cave on the far side of the island and vanished over the blue horizon. The Zentoria leader had escaped! Moments later the buried alien star craft and its adjoining base exploded deep underground. On the surface scientists recorded an impressive earthquake, but nothing else.

Chapter 29

In the cellar, they all emerged from the location jump and went sprawling on the floor in different directions. All except James who was still in his sitting position.

Mary sprang to her feet and ran around the cellar in confusion; finding herself in yet another strange location. She did not realise that they were under the family home! The others looked at her with silent amazement. Still trying to scream at the top of her voice she suddenly stopped and faced them, shaking her fists wildly.

"I still say you should leave her gagged all the time..." muttered TALON.

James smiled, for the first time in ages. "Tempting, but we had better beam her back up into the house above."

TALON muttered and changed the subject. "I wonder if she really is able to use your time suit, Master?"

James frowned, "Let's hope we never have to find out."

Davius nodded in agreement. "She saved us all, but it is better that she is returned to her parents and knows nothing of the quest."

Max completed its power-up and rose into the air. "But first I will bathe her in my amnesia ray and then put her to sleep."

Mary tried to shout again, furious that they were all talking about her as if she was not there! Desperately she tugged at the gag and tried to pull it free, determined to vent her fury on them.

Suddenly Max's big red eye turned yellow and it flooded her in a shimmering purple ray of light. She immediately stopped moving as if frozen. Her muffled rage ended and her eyes widened into a vacant stare. Max then rotated around her, performed more electronic wizardry and the gag dropped to the floor.

"She will remember nothing, but she needs to sleep for a while. You must location jump her up to the house now, James," instructed Max. The boy nodded, walked over and held her hand. He looked at her for a moment, and no longer viewed her as his infuriating older sister. Now she was someone who had saved his life. Then operating his controls they vanished in the blink of an eye. A moment later he reappeared, having left her asleep in her bedroom.

Sitting down on the cellar floor, James picked up the belt which Davius had been carrying. He lifted out each of the six crystals and put them in a small circle on the floor; each one touching the other.

"We could all do with a bit of healing..." he said with a heavy sigh.

"Be careful about using them all at the same time...!" warned Max; its eye flushed bright red.

The boy looked up, a scowl on his face. "Two things! Firstly I have purged myself of my evil side. Secondly I now realise that I can control the crystals at will. So don't interrupt me as I do this!"

Max floated back a few metres and gave way to the boy's assertive response.

From behind Max, Davius smiled and nodded in silent agreement; pleased that James was back in charge.

Touching each one, James coaxed a small portion of energy from each crystal, which appeared as a tiny pulsating light. Next he made each one rise into the air and merged them together into one quivering blob the size of a fist. Within the blob the colours swirled and mixed together like paint. Next he pointed at the blob and the merged energy separated into four shimmering, rainbow spheres of light the size of golf balls. Each one moved and hovered over James, Max, Davius and TALON. Next the energy balls showered each of them in droplets of light.

For a few minutes the rainbow light swirled around them; then finally the droplets faded away.

Fully re-energised, James calmly placed all the crystals into his belt and strapped it around his waist. Then without warning he sprang to his feet and pointed at the other three.

"Right, you lot; let's get our cards on the table!"

"You want to play cards?" muttered Davius confused.

"Table, what table?" added TALON equally confused.

Max floated higher into the chamber and opened its big eye very wide. "No, you idiots; he means that we put all our issues in the open and discuss everything honestly!"

"Damn right!" said James loudly.

Max started the confessions.

"Everything the Zentoria leader said is true. I am not from the future. I am the last of the race called the Metvals and I come from a planet light years from here. My aim was to enlist you to help me get the crystals to stop the Zentoria rebuilding their empire. I built TALON to locate the crystals. I am truly sorry that I had to trick you into helping me! The only experience I had of humans, was observing the treacherous ones who agreed to work secretly with the Zentoria. I thought that all humans were bad; but since meeting you I realise some humans can be good."

Davius stepped forward and began his statement.

"As the guardian of the Aquarius crystal I gladly gave it to you, James. I *still* fully support you. I confess that the Horoscope Matrix was secretly designed to prevent you from controlling the crystals because we feared that you would fall under their influence. Under the circumstances, I believe we were proved correct. However things have changed and you are now clearly able to control them safely."

TALON hovered from the floor and landed carefully on a work bench.

"All I know is that I still have the ancient coin inside me and I am ready to go and get the next crystal!"

James stepped forward, equally keen to discuss everything.

"I have something to confess to you, Max. On the mission to get the Aries crystal, I had to divert to get four ancient sheaths in order to save Davius's life. The four tasks I had to go on were even more far-fetched than anything I have done in our battles against the Dark Zodiac. Even Davius does not know what I had to do to get them. Even my own memory about the tasks is confused. It's as if I am supposed to forget how I got them!"

The High Priest straightened himself and continued where James had ended.

"The sheaths were secretly kept at the locations of the four power points of the British isles. Once James had got the sheaths from Silbury hill, Callanish, Bryn-celli-Ddu and New Grange I united them with their daggers at Stonehenge. The daggers were separated from the sheaths and brought from the four power points of the British Isles to rest in Stonehenge. They had been kept secretly hidden at Stonehenge for centuries. They were only to be re-united when the Isles were in their greatest peril. However I got James to get them as only their combined power was able to save me.

"Once their power had saved me, James and I came to the present time period. I left the four daggers and sheaths to be hidden by my priests at Stonehenge in my time period, where I assume they are still hidden even now. They should not be used again; unless the Isles are in danger!"

Max and James moved closer to the old man, willing him to say more.

"I now believe that they will be vital to winning a future battle! What is more I now believe that battle is the 'FINAL BATTLE' which my mystery ancestor mentioned when we were spying on him and James's ancestor in ancient Atlantis! *Even if James succeeds in battling to get all twelve crystals, the four daggers will be needed to win a thirteenth battle!*"

"So the quest has changed direction…" interrupted a bewildered TALON.

James sat down, keen to summarize and plan the next step.

"So, Davius and I are direct descendants of ancient Atlantis. Ten thousand years ago they hid the crystals to prevent them being captured, but left their locations on the coded coin. They also deliberately put the crystals in places to be discovered at key points in the world's history and recorded this on a stone tablet. The tablet also clearly identifies me as the person to undertake this quest. The tablet says so. The tablet also warns of that if I don't get them in strict order then human history will go catastrophically wrong. I was also destined to discover the black gas in the rocks, which enables me to time travel."

He put his head in his hands and sighed heavily then turned to face the others.

"However, it is clear from what Max has said that there is no future where the aliens have definitely taken over the world, so the outcome of this quest is still wide open for me to win!"

Chapter 30

"The quest is now clear!" interrupted TALON, keen to be off.

Max hovered into the centre of the room, urging caution.

"As James said, we must put all our cards on the table. We must be clear on the next steps. There are six more crystals to get; three earth signs and then three water signs. Each will mark a point in time where by going there James will *create* a key event in history.

"Just like the first six, they will all have guardians to be overcome. We must get them in the correct order and face the thirteenth battle; whatever it may be, when it comes. If it does involve the four daggers in some as yet unknown way, so be it."

"And what do we do once we have all the crystals?" questioned James, still slightly suspicious of Max. "Do we still destroy them, as you first ordered?"

"No, I will no longer deceive you, James. We must use them!" said Max assertively. "Once the twelve historic events have correctly taken place, the crystals must be used with the four daggers to win the final battle."

"And what about the Zentoria?" said Davius thoughtfully, "Will they still want to use the crystals to take over the world?"

Max thought for a moment, its memory banks recalling how its rival race had reacted to such defeats in the past.

"We destroyed their star craft and its adjoining base which was secretly buried under Easter Island. The Zentoria are now all extinct; except for their leader, who no doubt will have got away in some type of escape craft. Who knows where on earth it will have landed.

"It will also have taken with it the twelve zodiac clones, the time craft and any surviving robots. However it still does not know the location of the crystals, and the only way to get them is to track TALON."

TALON chuckled out loud, "And that will be difficult as their leader's body cannot withstand the physical pressures of time travel! That is why the Zentoria designed the time craft for the Dark Zodiac to use on their behalf!"

Max narrowed its eye, still processing data from its memory banks.

"TALON is correct. It will take some time for the Dark Zodiac to recover. We will finish the quest before they are able to strike again!"

James nodded and then stood up straight.

"It's just so difficult to take in what has been happening. So much so quickly! To visit a barren earth in the far future; then to see ancient Atlantis and learn that our ancestors come from there! Then to smash the Spanish Armada; helped by the Leo guardian! Then fighting intelligent dinosaurs, and stopping the Sagittarius guardian changing the course of evolution on earth! Then overcoming my dark and dangerous side permanently, and wiping out the aliens!"

He took a deep breath and let it out slowly. He stood tall and confident, like a great general about to lead his troops into battle. The meek schoolboy he was a few weeks ago was a distant memory.

"The original crystal quest is over. This is a new quest! We are a proper team once again! No more secrets or hidden plans. No more getting one crystal at a time and bringing it back here to go into the Horoscope Matrix!"

The others could feel a crackle of electricity beginning to build in the cellar, as the determination swelled in his voice. The crystals on his belt began to glow in response to his determination.

"The new quest is straightforward. It is a race to get the crystals first. From now on I will carry all the crystals I have with me, when we go and get the others. We overcome who, or whatever their guardians are. I now realise that I am being put through twelve tests of my character. We will only come back here once we have got them all and all the historic events have correctly taken place. When we return, we have to defeat the Dark Zodiac in a mysterious thirteenth battle to save the world. We will be victorious when we get the four daggers from Stonehenge and combine them with the crystals and use them as weapons against the enemy!"

The crystals around his waist glowed even brighter in response to his emotions.

The four of them suddenly felt a rush of excitement and fear, as James began to power-up his time suit.

"This is the start of a new quest. Let's go and get all the crystals now!"